P

"Tanith Lee writes 9

... ... *eekly*

"Tanith Lee is a ma ... ... disguise. *Electric Forest*, her latest venture, appears at first to be an offshoot of the classic Frankenstein, but just when you think you're on terra firma, Lee expertly pulls the rug out from under you. Don't miss this one." — *The Jackson Sun*

"Tanith Lee, again, shows her talent for writing a "can't put it down" book and shows that besides being a top-notch fantasy and science fiction writer, she is inventive as well. Highly recommended." — *Baryon Magazine*

"*Electric Forest* is more than an excellent novel—it is, in my opinion, one of the best works science fiction has so far produced, something I will reread for the rest of my life. . . . The story is gripping, the writing is excellent, the plot twists are dazzling—but even more, *Electric Forest* turns the reader inside-out, emotionally." — *Ares Magazine*

"This is the first Lee novel I've read and I'm impressed and delighted with her sensual style, her talents, and her mastery of language and narrative. There may not be one unnecessary word in this novel, and yet it is so rich and detailed and well-told that it arouses awe." — *Science Fiction Review*

"Skillfully written and richly imagined. . . . In this long and intricate epic, a large cast of humans struggle to attain their own ends and to escape their doom. Lee fans, and other admirers of the compelling tale, will be more than satisfied with the result." — *Booklist*

Electric Forest

TANITH LEE

DAW BOOKS, INC.

DONALD A. WOLLHEIM, FOUNDER

1745 Broadway, New York, NY 10019

ELIZABETH R. WOLLHEIM
SHEILA E. GILBERT
PUBLISHERS

www.dawbooks.com

First Paperback Printing, August 1979
First New Edition Printing, May 2019

1 2 3 4 5 6 7 8 9

TABLE OF CONTENTS

Pre-Screening:
Christophine del Jan
(This Presentation is Classified)

THE FOLLOWING DOCUMENT has been compiled from the data tapes, and prepared in narrative-descriptive form, in order to throw an ultimate light upon what took place between 10-4-1 and 9-1-2 of the Third Quarter, Blue and early Fall, Indigo.

Required reading can be, at this stage, irksome. I would ask, however, that you follow the manuscript on your screen in strict sequence, resisting the impulse to anticipate. After all, the motivation of the subject is the key element here, emotion and psychology providing clues to that motivation.

Nothing can be learned without some measure of risk, and, more vital still, of patience.

Additional material is naturally available via opto-con and audio. But this, too, I would ask you to delay using until the manuscript itself has been absorbed.

The screen is now at your disposal.

                                                                C.d.J.

One

Quarry and Hunter

I

UGLY STOOD ALONE before the processing machine.

The machine made certain types of cottene clothing, but Ugly never saw the syntho-cotton fed in at one tube above, nor the crisp white garments snowing out from the other below. Neither did she witness the actual metamorphosis that went on inside the machine in front of her. In the restricted space, three meters by two, Ugly stood alone with the processing machine and ran her stubby hands, clumsily but effectively, over the bank of green and red keys. It was simple to keep the machine functioning. The task should have left her mind free to think of other things.

Unfortunately, Ugly had very little to think about.

Ugly's shift comprised three hours on alternate days—five days a Dek; that was each oneday, threeday, fiveday, sevenday, and nineday. Every fifth Dek was free. For this program of work, Ugly received two hundred astrads each calendar month (four Deks), of which about one hundred and fifty went on accommodation, food, and essentials. Fifty astrads were nearly always left over to be spent on relaxation and pleasure.

Unfortunately, again, Ugly was not in an ideal position to spend them.

Ugly's name, of course, was not actually "Ugly." That was merely what most people—children, workmates—called her. It was not even a particularly cruel name any more, simply blisteringly accurate. No longer spoken in malice, it had lost some of its intrinsic offense—and gained some. Ugly herself had never commented on the matter, either way, nor on her real and registered name, Magdala Cled.

On any planet of the Earth conclave, fetal conception was the controlled result of selective, artificial impregnation. This ensured that all children born were healthy. Occasionally, however, mistakes occurred in the area of contraception, and a fetus was conceived biologically. Sometimes, such children were less than perfect. It had happened that Magdala Cled was one of these.

Her mother was a licensed prostitute; no one had bothered to identify her father. Intent on trade, the woman had forgone abortion until too late. She had subsequently dispelled her baby and dumped it, with the required five hundred astrads, on the State. Magdala had grown up in a state children's home.

A potential intelligence and interest had quickly submerged beneath regulation mechanical schooling that gave no outlet for speculation or the asking of even the most basic questions. It submerged, too, beneath the primitive malignancy of her fellow inmates, who (in their defense) were half-afraid of Magdala. For it was a society of regular features and well-formed physiognomy, and monsters were rare.

"Ugly!" the children screamed, as they tore Magdala's hair out, tripped her, stuck into her small sharp objects, pinched and kicked her. Almost as if, by constant assault, they could change her into something less dreadful.

But Magdala Cled, re-named Ugly, only grew uglier.

Just under one and a half meters in adult height, a great engine seemed to have descended upon her, squashing her downwards and sideways, and twisting her for good measure. Squat, square and irreparably leaning, Magdala walked with a sort of part-lagging, part-hopping step. From her skew shoulders, arms hung like afterthoughts, with spatulate afterthoughts of hands on them. And from her head, an afterthought of thin murky hair, chopped off at the neck. The modeling of the skull itself did show some mocking promise. Under other circumstances, it could have been the skull of an aware and creative woman. The face might have been poignant, though never pretty. But even that had not been possible for it. The flattened nose, the left eyelid which lay permanently almost closed on the gray-white cheek, had seen to that. Only the mouth was well-formed, though the teeth had broken long ago and been replaced by haphazard dental implants, shabby as the fate which had necessitated them.

Certainly, Magdala, in the most absolute sense, merited her second name. It suited her; she would have been the last to deny that.

Only inside her, never let out, the bewildered anger hid, the pain and fury. She hid them also from herself, when she could, did ugly Magdala.

On Earth Conclave planet Indigo, cosmetic surgery cost more astrads than a processory operative could save in seven years. Even the un-spendthrift Magdala. For there was not much call for such surgery, and the fee compensated. Besides, Magdala had only to glimpse herself in a reflective surface to know she would need more work upon herself than any physical human body could stand.

She was a hopeless case.

And if she thought about anything, as her stunted efficient fingers scrambled over the keys of her machine, ugly Magdala thought of that. A formless and useless sort of thinking, more like an ache in her brain than a thought. While sometimes superimposed upon the basic hopelessness was a list of that day's familiar miseries—the looks of strangers; pity and revulsion, the disgusted and desensitized looks of acquaintances (there were no friends).

And under it all, checked yet eternal, blazing anguish, howling.

At thirteen hours, Indigo noon, Magdala's shift finished. However, Magdala's relief was late, as her reliefs always were. Magdala, unprotesting, stayed at her post, until another girl slipped into the three-by-two cell.

"Thanks, Ugly," said the girl, and it was obvious she used the epithet now only as identification, no hurt consciously intended. "I guess I'm late again. Had to fix myself up." The girl was attractive, even in her cottene overall. She edged past Magdala and pressed at the key bank with an inch of raspberry nail. Her hair was the induced color of eighteen-carat gold, and she shook it contemptuously at the machine. "Three hours of this. Jesus. Still, I may be on the display benches next Dek."

Magdala stood in the cell doorway, watching the girl. Magdala's smeared plasticine face was quite illegible. The display benches had two-hour shifts only, and earned an extra fifty astrads per month, but, open to inspection, they were manned solely by the most good-looking men and women.

The golden girl yawned into a trap of raspberry nails.

"Go on, Ugly. Beat it. I'm expecting a bench supervisor by in a minute, and it's private."

Ugly left the machine cell, and made her stumbling exit along the corridor. Other machine cells opened off in the right-hand wall. On the left the lower extensions of solar generators thrummed. At the check point,

Magdala shed her overall into a disposal chute. Clad in her own shapeless utility garment, she sank in the elevator and emerged presently in the ozonized city air.

It was Blue, the season that on Indigo preceded Fall. On the shaved sloping lawns of the city the amber summer grass was turning the shade of wood-smoke; on the umbrella-formed trees along the sidewalks, the leaves hung like lapis lazuli. Above, the tall slender blocks of steel and glazium rose into a sky which was also intensely blue, and warm with the zenith sun of thirteen o'clock. A steady concerted vibration came from the city; the hum of solar generators at work on the high roofs and skylinks overhead, the purr of unseen vehicular traffic passing on the underground roadways. There was, too, the murmur of countless small devices—automatic sprinklers and fans, vendors, clocks, the gem-bright advertisements on the walls of occasional buildings, the faint regular throbbing of the live pavement at the sidewalk's center, and of a thousand elevators, moving stairs, reversible windows, sliding doors.

There were not many people aboard here in the commercial area of the city, for the thirteen-hour shift had checked out almost an hour before.

In the isolation, a handsome young man, passing on the slow outer section of the live pavement, glided by Magdala. His hair was pale and silken, and he was listening to music through the small silver discs resting lightly in his ears, but his eyes, wandering, alighted on the woman, and at once flinched frantically into reaction. Once or twice Magdala had caught a comment from those who were shocked by her appearance. "It's horrible. If I looked like her, I'd ask for work in one of the out-city plants." And another: "If *I* looked like that. I'd take enough analgens to see I didn't wake up." Magdala was accustomed to it all, the looks, the words. She seemed not to register them. Seemed not to.

Carried a short distance away, the pale-haired young man risked turning his head. Glazed in his web of externally noiseless music, he stared at Magdala, disbelieving.

Magdala did not use the live pavement. Even getting onto the slow outer strip proved difficult because of her awkwardness. And people did not like to travel with her, would wait till meters of the strip had gone by before they would step on in her wake. For this same reason she avoided the sub-transport, the sensit theaters, and most public haunts. She walked a great deal, on lonely thoroughfares, in her agonized, lurching fashion.

Six blocks from the clothing processory, the sidewalks opened into arcades and apartment-stores.

These could be the most unnerving moments of Magdala's journey, as, head bowed, gaze carefully blind, she fumbled through the periphery of the crowds. Sometimes people supposed her shortness to be that of a child, stopped to guide her, and recoiled in alarm. But today the arcades were not crowded and there were no incidents.

On the far side of the arcades lay an azure park where tame white or black doves fluttered about. Beyond the park towered seven Accomat blocks, in the fifth of which Magdala lived.

The Accomat was one of the cheapest ways to exist. Each apartment had a single main area three by four meters, with a bathroom cubicle half that size, and the normal accessories of food-dial, pay-dial and Tri-V screen, and limited furniture which unfolded from the wall. The perimeter variety also had windows. The inner did not, and here washed-air came through vents and second-hand daylight through refractors and shafts. Magdala's Accomat did not have a window.

The door shot wide in response to the pressure of her thumb in the print-lock. Magdala moved into the windowless, dim-lit, washed-air cell, just fractionally larger than the cell in which she worked. There was small evidence of her personality in this chamber, and what evidence there was had been cunningly concealed.

Now she did not hesitate, except for the constant physiological hesitation of her walk. She crossed to her pay-dial.

In answer to her index print, figures rose on the miniature screen. Today was pay day. Two hundred astrads had already been registered, and the rent, food bill, and tax on her apartment deducted and claimed by the Accomat computer. However, there was an impressive balance building up in her name at the central city bank. The figures showed just over five thousand astrads. She had only to index print and dial that figure to receive the corresponding check, which could then be cashed at any Bank Computer Station in the city. Instead, barely glancing at the screen, Magdala dialed a check for ten astrads.

On pay days, once a month, Magdala bought a meal in the Accomat Cafeteria. Once a month, that was thirteen times every year, Magdala slunk into the darkest corner booth of the bright and busy eating area, and ate the fresh meat, fresh vegetables, and fruit that the cafeteria could supply. The rest of the year, she relied on her food-dial, which dispensed plastic containers of revitalized frozen stuffs, vitamin capsules, and various fluids.

To visit the cafeteria, despite the dark booth, was nevertheless an ordeal. Generally, each restaurant served the inhabitants of its own apartment block, who were permitted to exchange and cash their pay-dial checks there, when ordering food. Most of the dwellers in the fifth block knew Magdala by sight, and scrupulously avoided her. Sometimes, however, outsiders would come in to eat, and they might see Magdala for the first time, registering the event explicitly.

The elevator sang gently as it flew like a bird up twenty stories.

Magdala stood in the elevator, her face its normal waxy blank. But even as her stomach tightened, aware of the coming meal, her mouth dried with an automatic inner cringing. She felt fear constantly but seldom revealed it, for she was used to being afraid, perpetually and instinctively tensed for the attitudes of the people about her. She often wished, positively and with no hint of childishness, that she might become invisible. Sometimes her fear rose to an extreme pitch. Otherwise, it merely breathed steadily within her, like the continuous steady breathing of the city.

The elevator stopped. Its door slid aside.

Magdala pulled herself out into the luminous sunlit space beyond, and began her arduous progress to the counter.

The two counter attendants leaned by the menu screen. One pointed Magdala out to the other. "Here's the cripple, like I said. She always comes in on processory pay days." She caught the words with ease. Swiftly she selected from the menu screen and the attendant tapped out her order to the mechanical kitchen. Magdala kept her eyes down. In this position, both lids drooping, her eyes seemed almost acceptable. The second attendant had submitted her ten-astrad check and returned now with her change. He skimmed it across to her, not touching her hand.

She was twenty-six. Since her birth, no one had ever willingly touched her, beyond the impersonal doctors at the state home and the children who had tortured her.

She took her tray and started toward the darkest booth. She was nearly there before she realized that someone was already seated inside.

Magdala was briefly confused. Today, the cafeteria was two-thirds empty and nobody took this booth when so many others, with access to the polarized sunny roof and glazium windows, were available. Then a new, more startled confusion overtook the first, for the seated figure in the booth was the pale-haired young man who had passed her on the street.

His profile, blond like his hair against a somber ground, was so fine, so perfectly made, it seemed machine finished. The long-lashed eyes shone translucent yet metallic. A glazium beaker of red alcohol on the table before him had been encircled by a notable, hard, flexible, and long-fingered hand, that appeared almost alive of its own volition. The silver music discs were no longer inside his ears.

Magdala threw her body hurriedly into retreat, commencing the turn which would carry her to safety.

"Don't run away."

Magdala halted in the midst of her turning, listened for what would come next. Nothing came.

Magdala completed the turn and assayed a step.

"Why do you persist in running away, when I just told you not to?"

The voice was cool and virtually expressionless.

Again Magdala had involuntarily halted. She did not look about. She sensed rather than saw the young man, full face to her now, waiting, his arm casually draped across the back of the booth.

"Sit down," he said.

Something galvanized Magdala. She was able to move again, and did so. He said nothing further as she walked gradually along the line of vacant booths.

She was not sure why her fear had sharpened with such vehemence. Surprise, maybe. Perhaps this man was one of those who sometimes burst out into speech with her, sickly fascinated into uncontrolled conversation. But he had not spoken in that way at all. And control did not seem to be, at the moment, his problem.

Magdala entered a booth and laid out her tray. Her wrists were trembling. She put a mouthful of food between her lips, chewing carefully. When the mouthful had been swallowed, she introduced another.

She had been eating for five minutes when his shadow fell across her tray.

He moved around the table and sat down facing her.

This time, her eyes flickered once over his face. She could not help that. Then she dropped her head lower over her plate. She kept eating, but she could not taste the food. He sat, immobile, watching.

Long ago, she had been warned that she might meet those who took an unwholesome interest in her condition. Those who might wish to harm her, eradicate her—

From three or four short glimpses, he had been recorded in great detail on her retina. The bleach-colored hair appeared natural, and naturally striped through with curious subsidiary streakings: dun, gold, gray. The eyes, seen close to, like the hair were multitudinously blended, striped, flecked, which amalgam, from a short distance, formed two extraordinary lenses of polished greenish brass.

His proximity was truly terrifying. Not because of any previous warning. Not even because of his frightening uniqueness. But because of some unseeable, totally lethal thing. As if he were radioactive.

"What's your name?"

His voice had not altered. Still cool, unhurried and flat.

Magdala ate, eyes on the food.

"I said, what's your name?"

Magdala ate, and found she could not swallow.

"What's the matter? Are you afraid of me? There's no need."

Magdala managed to swallow. She had had to, she wanted to say something. She said: "Please leave me alone."

"I want to know your name," he said.

"Why?" Now that she had communicated with him, it was difficult to resume silence.

"You won't tell me your name because you're patently afraid to. But, as you see, I followed you from the commercial area, and a minor inquiry led me to anticipate your visit here, even your chosen booth. I can probably locate your apartment as simply. In fact, withholding your name won't prevent me from discovering as much about you as I wish."

Magdala dragged herself along the seat and upright. Leaving her meal unfinished, she walked toward the elevator. She could not travel fast. Any moment she expected his shadow to slant again across her path, his inexorable voice to jerk her to a standstill. He could catch up to her with no trouble. But he did not.

She entered the elevator with several men and women who were vacating the cafeteria.

Between their bodies, and across all the sun-glowing tangle of booths, tables, and human movement, she saw his beautiful and horrifying face staring straight back at her. And even as the door slid to and the singing elevator dropped softly toward the earth, his face remained, painted upon the skin of the air.

II

SHE WALKED ALONG the edge of the park, keeping to those spots where trees and plants were most thickly massed. From inside a tunnel of shadow, she gazed out and beheld the park dotted sparsely by people, swimming in the pool, feeding the black and white doves. Later, she walked through the narrow back streets, behind the blocks of old stores, second-hand precincts of curios and paper books, virtually deserted. For two hours she read in a cubicle at the electro-library. They were used to her there, and offered no comment. But as the machine whispered the pages into view on the screen, she barely saw them.

The warm blue day began to roll downhill into a fiery sunset behind the slender glazium towers. Like a firework display on the crimson sky, a million little green shocks emitted from the high roofs and the upper links as the solar generators of the city closed their circuits against the night.

Under the igniting street lights and checkerboard of blank yellow or black windows, Magdala, a ghastly lurching shape, moved homeward along the boulevards.

The elevator carried her to her floor. Her door dashed

wide at the touch of her thumb. Before she could check herself, she had entered her apartment. Windowless, it should therefore be black now as a hole in the ground, till her entry triggered its lamps. But the apartment was already full of light, its lamps already triggered. And in the center of the light, like its sun and its source, stood the man.

Somehow, she had known. Known that, impossibly, he would be waiting for her here. Not once during her afternoon wandering had she glanced over her shoulder. Not once had her fear risen to its extreme pitch, out on the street.

Yet no stranger could enter through a print-lock, a lock whose function was to respond to one print alone: that of its owner.

The young man showed Magdala a silver rectangle lying in his hand.

"It's not magic," he said. "This takes a sensor-reading of your print from the lock. I press the little switch, and the reading is played back into the lock. The lock obeys. Earth Conclave government has possessed similar gadgets for years. Nothing is to be relied on, M. Cled. Believe me."

Omnipotent, he had discovered her name. He must have asked one of the Accomat staff, then located her apartment number from the registration screen in the foyer. He had been very thorough, very determined.

Behind her, the door had automatically shut. In the tiny, near-featureless room, he blazed and burned like a star. She could not take her eyes off him finally, staring up at him, hypnotized, her brain struggling.

"Magdala," he said musingly, "Magdala Cled. Let me see. Cled is a composite name, is it not? Your mother's initials, or your father's, or a combination of both, preceded by C, the initial of the State Orphanage where you were brought up. Am I right? Magdala, however.

Now that *is* interesting. Let me hazard a guess. Your mother was a licensed whore, and State Orphanage C had a reformatory whim. Yes, that would have to be it. Mary of Magdala, the repentant prostitute of Modernist Christianity."

Magdala had not properly listened to what he was saying. A part of her was convinced that he had come here to kill her and would now do so. She waited, desperate, dazzled; numbed by lack of resolution.

But he made no move toward her. The reverse. He buttoned down one of three folding seats from the wall, and sat on it. Idly, he threw the silver door opener up into the air, caught it. Threw it, caught it.

"I suppose," he said, soft as cold snow falling on her mind, "you think I am a horrible maniac, bent on removing every last crippled lady from Indigo. I'm not, dear hideous crippled lady, anything of the sort."

Magdala's twisted shoulders met the wall. She pressed herself against it. "Please," she said, "please go away."

"We've been through that before. Obviously, I've no intention of going away. You can assume I want something from you. Why don't you amuse us both by guessing what it is?"

"Cash," she said. Her heart surged. "I'll dial it for you. Five thousand astrads. Then you can go."

"How interesting. Yes, that's a possibility. But don't worry. I could fix your pay-dial as easily as I did the door. If I wanted your astrads, I'd have gotten them already. So that eliminates theft and murder. What else would it be? Perhaps I'm a pervert aroused only by the obscenely unwholesome. Sorry, your luck's out. Not that, either."

"Please—" she said again.

"I suggest you stop pleading with me to go. Don't you like me? Don't you think I'm rather decorative? Most people do."

She had edged all the way along the wall. Her right foot rested over the plate in the floor that worked the door from the inside. But the door did not open.

"Yes, I've tampered with that, too. I'm clever as well as ornamental, you see."

Suddenly, he ran his hand down the button panel next to his seat. Instantly, all the furniture unfolded from the walls. The two other seats, the couch, the table, the cabinet with its magnetized shelves. The room was jammed by a mob of white plastic fitments. And thus revealed in the midst of it, were the hidden aspects of Magdala.

She understood that he had already done this once, earlier, before she returned. He had seen everything. The twenty paperback books, the minute desk of music cassettes, the limpid seashell from Sapphire Flats, the jade bead from Earth. And on the bed, somehow more naked than anything else, the sleek-furred simulate cat—a child's toy.

His eyes flickered over her secrets, registered the imprint of her soul, just as the cunning device had registered her thumb print in the lock. Then he rose, picked delicately between the unfolded furniture, and lifted her toy cat by its forepaws.

"So it's true," he remarked, "we all need something to love."

To get between the furniture was harder for Magdala, but she succeeded. Reaching him with a quickness that surprised both of them, she flung up one hand to seize the cat. The other she drove against his ribs. She had not been tortured by children without learning from them, and her spatulate hand appeared to hurt him a lot. He swung aside in the narrow space with a ragged gasp of pain.

Nevertheless, she became aware in that moment that he had provoked her for his own reasons, and that she had followed his leads as he must have predicted to himself she would.

She stood with the toy cat in her arms, betrayed into self-revelation.

"Congratulations," he murmured, "you're human." He passed one long hand rhythmically across his side, where she had jabbed at him. "I was beginning to wonder. You don't, of course, *look* human. I expect you'd like to. Would you?"

She had crossed some peculiar line within herself. Her voice came from her throat, rough and strong: "Would I like what?"

He half-turned, and demagnetized one of the paperbacks. He opened a page, and held up before her the photoplate of the long-limbed Venus, her underwater flesh folded in yellow hair.

"How would you like," he said distinctly, "to be beautiful?"

Her heart stopped. Laughter began instead. She had never really laughed before in her life. Somewhere in the middle of this laughter, she lifted the white shell from its shelf, raised it above her head, and cut with its pointed cusp at the young man's face.

Whether he expected this second blow was not clear. Frantically he deflected it, his arm darting to protect his face. The point of the shell slit his hand. The impact whirled the shell aside. It brushed the wall and broke in fragments.

Magdala's mouth, mobile with laughter, contorted and closed. She regarded the broken shell, her eyes swelling as if to cry, yet without moisture. The habit of tearlessness prevailed. When he lifted his uninjured hand and struck her across the head, she rocked back, righted herself like some grotesque rubberized doll. She had braced herself for his retaliation and took no interest in it.

And then, a bizarre dawning of amazement filled her. Physically, although in violence, they had touched.

Blood dripped from his skin. He was gray. It came

home to her, a profound truth, that he loved his own looks, and feared greatly to be robbed of them.

"I take it from your display," he said, "that the thought of being beautiful does capture your imagination, somewhat." His voice was shaking, no longer cool or flat.

"You can't alter me," she said. "No one can." His shaking voice, his youth (a little younger than she, perhaps?), his very flawlessness, gave her abruptly a sense of power. After all, she was the one with nothing to lose. "Besides," she said, "I have only five thousand astrads. It costs a lot, surgery. Are you a medic? Is that it?"

But then he smiled again, and her brief confidence abandoned her. His smile was like a white door sliding ajar upon an alien world.

"I'm not a medic. Nor do I require your pathetic astrads. I'm rich, dearest revolting Magdala. And I can make you beautiful."

"You're crazy," she said.

"Beautiful," he repeated. "Beautiful. Beautiful."

They stood and looked at each other in a long and utter quiet.

III

BEYOND THE CITY, the blue-pastel morning mist of Indigo's Blue season lay thick and sweet-smelling over twenty sweeping highways of concrete and shining steel. Here, by day, the traffic ran above ground, fast, driverless auto-buses and fish-gleaming cars. The highways waited for dawn, noiseless under the fragrant fog.

At six-o'clock the sun began to rise, and the first auto-bus of the morning, jeweled in a constellation of lights, raced down the western freeway.

Blue through the blue mist filter, the world illusorily fled from the bus. Flying embankments fringed by trees with sun-sketched limbs and speed-smoking crests. Far away, dim blocks and domes, the out-city refineries and plants, their hydro canals like bubbling glazium. And now the rush of a golden rocket, a passing bus flinging itself cityward in the opposite direction. The deformed woman, crouched at her window, watched it all.

Her scanty fellow passengers were indifferent, even to her, it seemed.

Some had inserted in their ears the enamel discs that connected to the tape-music of the bus. Some slept.

The bus stopped twice in the initial fifty kilometers.

The third regulation stop, one hundred and forty kilometers from the city, loomed up sharply solitary by the highway. Around the stop poured merely a landscape, uncultivated and oddly primeval in the levelly climbing sunlight and the evaporations of the mist.

Moments after Magdala had descended, the bus was gone along the highway, melting into the vast azure parasol of the morning.

Presently, she went into the stop shelter, and seated herself.

Apart from the road, nothing man-made was visible—neither complexities of buildings nor any further traffic. Trees had spilled close across an eastern rise. Magdala, accustomed to the perpetual purring of the city, listened to the trilling of winds and the faint cry of birds in the wood. The novelty of these sounds combined in a frightening ambience with the novelty and strangeness of her situation. Anything might happen.

The happening occurred.

A silver mote materialized on the eastern horizon, became a shooting flame like light running over silk. A great silver car, like an incredible aqueous beast, swam to a halt beside her.

She stared at the car until, impatient, it roared at her from some bronze vocal-apparatus within. Then she got up and went to it meekly. She carried no bags, was empty-handed as she had been instructed to be.

He sat at the wheel, intolerant of the robot-drive. Pale as ice, he looked at her without friendship through the wine-dark polarization of the windscreen.

"Get in," he said. The rear side section lifted to admit her. Awkwardly, Magdala hauled herself into the ozonized interior. "How many saw you?"

"The people on the bus. No one I ever met."

"And you brought nothing with you? No astrads?"

"No."

"And not your toy cat, I trust."

She did not answer. He could observe she had followed his instructions. "We must make you seem to vanish," he had said, carelessly, imperiously. "Ugly Magdala, disappearing into thin air. You'll like that, won't you?" So her bank-balance had been left uncashed, and her possessions had been left in her apartment. No statement of absence had been sent to the processory, no statement of vacancy to the Accomat. Nothing. She had made her exit before sunrise, mostly unwitnessed.

She had not questioned his insistence on deceit. Perhaps he meant to kill her after all. Was this just his joke, with death at the end?

She thought of the shell, and lunging at his handsome face with it. His shaking voice, her fatalistic brief grasping of power.

Today, he was expensively dressed. Today, she could see he was rich. There was not even a mark on his hand where the shell had torn him: he could buy the best cosmetic sealing ointment on the market.

He touched a button in the dash panel. The car seared into an avid vibrancy of life, and slipped forward into motion as into water. Once more the world was sent reeling off from her.

In fearful stupid pleasure, she watched it go.

"My name is Claudio Loro. It intrigues me that you've never asked. You have none of the veneer of social behavior, do you, Magdala? When we reach the city state line, in about fifteen minutes from now, I want you to get into the seat-storage compartment and let me seal you in. Otherwise, they'll ask your reason for crossing through with me, and you don't really know what it is, do you?"

They had been traveling west then north for three

hours. He had not spoken to her before. The silver discs were in his ears; sometimes he sang to the unheard melody in his head. His voice was beautiful, effortless, contemptuous, and banal. Magdala had exhaustedly dozed, lulled by his voice and the flight of the big car.

The city state line ended at the river. Beyond, old precolonial roads splayed between the hills. The industrial and urban development of the city had not moved in this direction yet. Far over the hills lay Sapphire Flats, with its outplanet independent research stations, its resorts and fish farms, and a sapphire northern sea boiling on its shores.

When he buttoned up the back seat, she climbed gracelessly into it and he closed her inside. But a muted lighting came on, and washed-air bathed the compartment. All the while, she had had intimations that she was part of some plan of his, that it was the plan which demanded stealth. And here was proof in this preparation and concealment. She was to be his experiment. He meant no one else to know of it, which indicated the experiment was dubious, probably illegal, possibly fatal. But the slow internal music of her fear played only softly. She did not really care. She did not really care that she was shut into the rear seat, that she was in danger, that she sensed his madness like the ozone in the atmosphere. Without her, he would founder. *She* had generated all this action. That was her true power over him. Over *Claudio*.

When they paused at the city state line check point, she heard muffled voices, a few words, but it appeared no one wanted to examine the car. Fortunate for Claudio? But then, the car was the undisputed possession of a rich man, an exquisite extension of Claudio himself. Only the human thing under the seat would have marred his image, had it been discovered.

Soon, the vehicle sprang forward into the subway

beneath the river. But they were ten kilometers into the hills before he let her out of the storage compartment.

Shortly after releasing her, he gave her an eliminex lozenge, the high classification drug which negated the functional needs of elimination for up to twenty-five hours. She pondered incuriously how he had got hold of it. "I don't intend to stop for anything else," he said. "I've wasted enough time. I've wasted two years, did you but know it, my haglike passenger."

During the afternoon they ate from a food-dial and drank wine, blue-bloomed as its parent grapes. The car, switched to robot-drive, sped along the ancient asphalt roads on its pre-programmed course.

She did not ask him anything, not even their destination. He told her nothing. Once or twice he spoke to her, a comment on the swirling terrain beyond the windows, or an instruction. She obeyed his instructions. Tense, she traced his comparable tension, ticking in the car. Never in her life before had she shared anything with anyone.

Even if he killed her, they would share her death.

She had no measure by which to judge either his behavior or her reactions to it. Like the speed of the car, this thing bore her with it. She no longer knew whether she was afraid or glad.

They had driven for thirteen hours, when night came down like a leisurely black shutter. Unveiled by city lights, stars blazed, uncountable white holocausts against the black.

The road dropped suddenly, the hills divided. Full in the single broad headlamp of the car, Magdala saw a blue salt beach cascading to the jaws of the sea.

Only in a sensit theater, long ago, had she ever beheld the sea, tasted its winds, touched her feet in its coldness. The sensit had faded. Reality stunned her. The sea was the sky, but the sky in motion. A flung shawl of breakers smashed the stars all over the shore.

The car kept on, speeding parallel to the bay.

A high wall came from the dark beyond the lamp and the car eased its pace. Seven seconds passed as Claudio held down a key on the dash. Then the wall opened and the car leaped through.

They plunged deep among trees, toward a thing which shone. There was a house within the wall. An old house, three stories high, a house that was a metallic brick. Soft as fall rain, the starlight slithered on its mercurialized cladding, where no windows showed. A faceless house, shining amid trees, amid the pale hoarse bellowing of the ocean.

"Get out," Claudio said to her, just as, thirteen hours before, he had said, "get in."

They stood on a driveway, and the car sank into the earth on a slice of steel, and the driveway joined over it. The night was wind-blown, but the trees about the mercury house never shivered.

There was no print-lock. They waited there as the house woke within itself, recognizing Claudio by autocular mechanism. When it was satisfied, it let them in.

Dawn began to flood the house immediately when they entered. The illumination came by delicate degrees, flushing rouge-gold through the walls, heightening, brightening, till the ceiling was suffused.

Claudio removed the music discs from his ears and threw them away. The air seemed to catch them, lower them into a catchment of air. They settled on a table like blown leaves.

"Magnetic beams," he said, "and the light's a sunrise fitment. I mentioned I was rich. More?" He stroked a panel, and the walls were gone. The sea and the night plastered their black fires over the room. Each whole wall was a one-way reversible window, invisible from outside. "Rich and—did I say?—clever. Don't you think I'm clever, Magdala? But you have yet to see the cleverest thing of all."

His expensive whiteness gleamed in the house. He was so right for the house. He led her on to a velvet carpeted ramp which bore them upward. He operated gadgets en route, the show pieces of the house, but his face was frigidly set. Pink snow showered; a fountain glittered without fluid or substance. Portions of walls spread and retracted like the petals of flowers in a solarium.

"Two years," Claudio said. "Wasted. I used to go hunting, searching. For someone like you, my Magdala. But you're unusual, my dear. A freak. Hard to come by. And it had to be someone like you. A genetic mistake. An atrocity, crawling about its hopeless round. Devoid of normal self-preservative wariness. Mewing, inside its warped little soul, for rescue. Not quite human. Here we are." The ramp had drifted them up to the third story and grown still. He gripped her clumsy paw in his well-made icy hand. A door shifted for them. They walked into a small white area.

A panel of keys and unlit lights was set in one wall.

Between the panel and the door, a cloudy crystal pillar, two meters high.

"Prepare yourself," Claudio whispered. His eyes were watering slightly, nervously, as if with tears.

Magdala said nothing. The song of her fear had mounted, but she seemed divorced from it. She seemed, indeed, alone on a huge markerless plain. Even fear could not keep her company there. And the man at her side was like a prologue to the voice of a storm. To the voice of God.

He crossed to the pillar and did something to it. The crystal started to uncloud.

"Yes," he said, "look at her all you want."

There was a woman in the pillar. She would appear

to be about twenty-two or three years of age. She would appear to be *alive*, but surely could not be. Naked, she was like some glowing incandescent substance. Her open eyes were dark blue neons. Lustrous hair, a fierce blue essence of blue-black, altogether nearly more blue than black, almost navy in color, poured back from her forehead. The hair was cut precisely level with her shoulders, the heavy, mathematically straight mass of it just framing their witness. But she was not any sort of a mannequin. She had nails, lashes, a fine bluish blush of down beneath her navel, leading into black at the pubes. The fawn nipples on her breasts were like furled buds. And she was dusted all over with a pollen of faint fawn freckles. She was beautiful. Beautiful.

"Yes," Claudio murmured again. "Look all you want, Magdala. Memorize her. This is what you are going to be."

Two

Venus Rising

I

IN THE DAY TIME, the mercurialized cladding of the house burned up in a drastic dry white fire. The tall trees that massed about it inside the wall seemed to make vain attempts to douse the fire with their blue stems. But there was something wrong with the trees. Tactile, fertile, conveying vague drifts of scent, they grew in the unnourishing rock of the shore above the salt flats of the salty sea. When their blue leaves fell, which sometimes they did, it was not in answer to the wind and Magdala could not afterward find the leaves upon the ground. And when the blaze of the house or of the sun itself moved behind them, the trees dissolved. The trees were not real.

She was still dutiful to Claudio's commands. He had commanded her to sleep and handed her a pill to enable her to do so. She had swallowed the pill and slept. This morning he had told her to walk among his trees. She had come out and walked. Soon he would call her to go in, and she would do that also. Then terror would begin, but she would continue to obey him. Through all the terror.

He had shown her. Terror had come then, too. When

he had told her his plan (without explanation): terror. But not terror alone. The buried anguish had gushed to the surface of her brain, her anger and her bitter, bitter despair. And from the depths of her, in the wake of these emotions, a scream of passionate demand.

She had no reason not to believe in the impossible. Desperation was always ready to pray for miracles.

He called her. By some sophisticated system of loud-hailer, she heard his voice, evenly pitched and modulated, as if he stood at her side.

"It's time, Magdala."

She returned, through the unreal, millionaire's holo-stetically projected trees, toward the fiery furnace of the house.

The glazium capsule was one and three-quarter meters long, one and a half meters around. It rested slightly backward, tilted at a thirty-degree angle by an arrange-ment of the flexium steel support which had lowered it into position through the ceiling of the white-walled room. The capsule had been opened, then closed, and to its transparent exterior had been affixed the panel of keys and unlit lights, detached entire from the wall. A variety of wires and connecting leads proceeded from the apparatus in the capsule and passed, via apertures in the glazium, through into this panel. The apparatus itself cradled the distorted form of Magdala Cled.

"Can you hear me?" Claudio asked her.

She nodded.

"Shall I describe the picture you present?" he said. "A nightmare by Bruegel. Have you heard of Bruegel? Never mind."

It was comfortable inside the capsule, despite the tubes and coils, the things which had been attached painlessly and intimately to her, the delicate cage which clasped her skull. He had seen to everything with absolute indifference, keeping up, nevertheless, a cruel rhetorical banter. He detailed for her, meticulously, her ugliness. Contrastingly, he reassured her she would not be hurt. "Nothing to cut or slash," he said sweetly. "I am a scientist, not a surgeon."

The creature in the crystal column watched them sightlessly all the while from her blue neon eyes. These eyes, never blinking, never shut, remained limpid. Claudio had let Magdala look closely. She had seen the minuscule pores in the skin, the tracery of veins. Then he had raised the column and guided Magdala's hand to the flesh itself and the navy hair.

"I said I was clever," he kept reiterating. But he himself did not handle the warm satin flesh. "You would swear she was alive," he said. "Static but animate." But he had already told Magdala that the woman was not alive and not animate. Every part of her had been constructed, in a tank, by hand and by machine, by his hands and his machines. Yet you stroked her and saw her and breathed the carnal perfume of her, and forgot.

"*Not*, my dear Magdala, a mechanized robot. Not that mythical being, an android. Decidedly not human. Like you, my ugly one. A freak."

After that, he let down again the crystal cylinder, trapping his creation like an orchid under glass.

Magdala lay in the capsule, and the unwoman gazed through her. Drugs had quieted Magdala's nerves and organs to an analgesic sponge. Her drugged terror was theoretic, meaningless. Magdala stared in return in the blue neon eyes.

"Yes," he said. "Number her freckles, the hairs of her head."

Then he pressed the master switch of the panel. All but one key responded. The lights exploded into many colors.

Magdala felt a new thing. Far off and anesthetized, the

action of the attachments and wires upon her and within. Her cradle, now alert, would feed her, evacuate her, breathe for her, at certain times stimulate and exercise her limbs, her heart, lungs and intestines. The little glittering tubes, sipping and nurturing, cossetting, nursing, would maintain indefinitely her supine framework, in perfect health. She was giving herself over to the most tender care (his words). Her cradle would treat her better than she had ever treated herself. And better, much better, than the intemperate world. And now she could say goodbye to herself. To her deformed, flattened, and twisted body. She was no longer responsible. She was leaving home.

"Are you ready?" he said. His pale face through the glazium glared in at her. He, too, was afraid, presumably, playing God. Doing it more successfully than God.

She inclined her head once more.

(Surely his promises were lies. He was mad. She would die. He the murderer, she the consenting victim, mesmerized by his madness.)

He grinned and pressed the last key down into the panel.

He had warned her. It was worse than the warning.

Fires rained through her head and went out. Catapulted into nothing, she fought to regain her equilibrium, fought to regain her body. The urge was instinctive. In the blind and infinite ocean of un-ness, she screamed without a voice. Had he killed her? Was this her death?

Then his voice came through the deaf clamor of breakers.

"No," he said. "*No*. Do as I told you. *Do* it."

She struggled, toward the shore now. She knew the shore. She had been shown it, had caressed it, breathed in it.

She broke the surface of the sea. He had not lied.

As if from a great distance, she saw again his face—livid and horrified. She watched it change, grow whiter, yet relaxing, relaxing to the point of flaccidity, becoming idiotic. She knew why. Confronting the woman under the crystal pillar, he had seen her blink.

Magdala blinked a second time.

Carefully, uncertain, she moved her right hand to meet the switch inside the cylinder. Her right hand was graceful, beautiful. Freckled. She felt the impression, finger-tip on switch, felt it exactly. The cylinder rose.

"My God," he said. "Pygmalion."

He was laughing. Then abruptly he turned and went out. She heard him start to vomit before the rush of running water smothered it.

She remained motionless, afraid to take a step till he came back.

Presently he returned, and sat on the floor, leaning his spine against the wall. He looked sick still, and still amused.

"Say something," he suggested.

She had to think to make her lips open. Then no sound would come.

"Goddammit, orient yourself. I've told you how."

She thought of speaking. She could speak. Draw a breath, let the breath hit the voice box. Let her lips shape a sentence. She spoke.

"It isn—n't easy."

She had never heard this voice before, this lovely cinnamon voice. She filled her lungs that were not lungs.

"I want to see," she said, "I must see myself."

"Oh frailty," he said, "thy name is woman. Get down off your pedestal then, and I'll conduct you to a mirror."

She began to walk to him, faltering. She was helplessly trying to walk in her accustomed way, the old way, sidling, hopping, dragging, lurching.

"No!" he shouted at her. He jumped up. He ran forward. Her eyes were level with the hollow beneath his lower lip. It shocked her, her height, as the sensation of the

switch to her finger had shocked, the floor under her feet.
She supposed he might strike her, his negligible patience
already exhausted. But he did not. He pulled up short of
her. "You are a woman now," he grated. "Walk like a
woman." She took stock of herself. Thinking each step,
she walked. "It improves," he said. "You've got a long way
to go." He came round her then, and placed his hand on
her ribs beneath her left breast. This was the final shock
of touch; nothing inanimate could shock her more than
his human palm and fingers wrapped about her. "Heart
beat," he said. "Everything works." He moved his hand
away and saw it trembling. "Now, a mirror."

They walked past the capsule. She did not glance at it
and she could see he kept note of her avoidance. He led
her along a corridor into a large room. The room was
five-sided, one transparent wall looking out across the
holostet trees to the wild blue waves dashing below in the
bay, and four walls that became mirrors at the contact of
his hand beside the door.

"This is your schoolroom," he said. He hesitated on
using her name, "Magdala. You will learn most of your
lessons in here, with the loving aid of a looking glass.
Practice."

By the time he reached the door, his neurasthenic
trembling was strongly evident. He went out, the door
slid shut, and left her alone with herself.

Or, with the self she had become.

II

S HE LEARNED.
Without completely comprehending, still she learned. She could mislay the memory of her other primal self, as moment by moment, she became what she saw in the mirrors.

Hours passed. She moved in a dream, a beautiful dream, like certain somnolent fantasies she had had in childhood. . . . Subliminally, she prepared to wake up, for the dream to shatter. She did not wake. The dream went on.

It was sunset, pink sky over blue water through the wall window. The sunset smoothed the savage coast, stained all the mirrors. Rather than waking, she had fallen asleep among her reflections.

She had speculated, but now, amazed into objectivity, she questioned that this un-human body could lose its senses. Robot—machine—synthetic simulacrum—whatever it was, how could it *sleep*?

A voice sang in the wall: *Play me.*

She turned. One of the mirrors had opaqued. A silver disc pulsed softly. *I am a recorded tape. Play me*, repeated the voice.

Incidental to her contemplation, she had happened on various tricks of the room. How all the walls and the window could be altered to other things—plastase silk, electrobook screen, trivision receiver, multicolored kaleidoscope. A chute brought food from a service unit in the kitchen below. A panel lifted to reveal a sea-shade bathroom. . . .

Play me! whined the tape machine.

She reached to depress its button. Her movements generally commenced naturally now, changing halfway as awareness of what she did unbalanced her into confusion. This is not *myself*. This is—

Play me!

She pressed the button into its socket, and Claudio's voice, calm and accurate as a machine itself, emanated from the disc.

"Listen, Magdala, and listen assiduously. I have recorded this especially for your benefit. And mine. I don't want to give you the data, face to face. It would bore me. It would, I admit, disturb me. To look at you, and explain you to yourself. Because you are yourself now. There'll probably never be any occasion for you to revert to what you were before, that thing lying in the maintenance capsule. You can disown that, even if you won't ever quite be able to ignore it. Are you listening? Don't let your mind wander. I am going to tell you everything I consider you should know about your unique condition. Concentrate. This relates to your survival."

She obeyed. Obedience was a nearly foolproof method of coping with both the situation and the man.

"I'll put it into simple terms. You won't understand it otherwise, will you? And you have to understand. You can't survive unless you do. Let me explain the phenomena itself, first. My God, it occurs to me that perhaps you have religion, Magdala, Modernist Christianity or Totalism. If that's your problem, you'll presume I've trans-

ferred your animus—your soul—from one body to
another. Well, if you presumed that, erase it. You haven't
actually gone anywhere—not soul, not even mind. You're
still imprisoned, in point of fact, within that lump of foul
accidental composition in which I located you. So what's
different? It's your *consciousness* that's been shifted.
That and that alone.

"I'll give you an analogy. It's fair. It may help you. A
dream. You lie asleep, tissues, bones, blood, organs,
brain, complete and in the same place. But the dreaming
faculty of your mind convinces you you're elsewhere.
Your body stays where it is, but your dream insists you
are what?—possibly swimming in a cold ocean. Second
analogy, better than the first—the sensit. You enter a
crowded theater, put a headset on, and the sensit puts
you, cerebrally, into a desert. You experience the sand,
the hot winds, you smell the dust. Dream or sensit, that
other place seems real. It isn't, but it seems to be. And
that's what's happening to you now, Magdala, your consciousness has transferred wholly from your own un-
lovely head to a crystal conductor in the skull of a
simulate woman. It's a sensit dream, but, Christ, the
most fantastic sensit of them all, because this is *real*.
You've got a body that factually will be doing whatever
you experience. You've got a body that will come to follow your neural instructions as instinctively and as
swiftly as your physical body did. While your physical
body will perform none of these actions, will lie quiescent in its capsule. It doesn't need much from you now,
that physical body. It's just the powerhouse, the brain
that provides your consciousness with its life. But you
can't turn it off, any more than any other powerhouse.
You can't forget it. You can't abandon it. It's the last and
only millstone around your neck. It's a symbiote, a ben-
eficial parasite. You can't get by without it.

"Here are the facts. Once every eight days, each

eight-day cycle to the hour, you will have to visit your capsule. The capsule has its own self-servicing equipment, but certain fluids must be re-stimulated, and various accretions dissipated. Once every eight days. You will find comprehensive instructions on the side of the capsule. The process is minimal and uncomplicated, merely the pressing of a few buttons. It is, however, vital. Your body supports your brain. *Mens sana in corpore sano*, at its most uncompromising. If the body deteriorates, so does the brain, and without your brain, your consciousness cannot operate. From now on, Magdala, you are a beautiful woman with an imbecile child. A nurse attends to this child, but every eighth day your assistance with the brat is called for. Otherwise, you are free to do as you wish. You can even travel—the capsule is stabilized to survive accepted forms of transport, since it must accompany you on any prolonged journey. It's the one piece of luggage you can't leave behind. I'm sure you appreciate that.

"The last section of data is probably so obvious it doesn't demand explanation. Nevertheless, I'll explain it to you. I developed this miracle. Perhaps I'm too facile with it. You won't be. Yet. Your new body is equipped with an entire assembly of simulate parallels—heart, lungs, intestinal organs. Your eyes blink automatically; similarly your heart beats and you breathe. You can eat and drink, too, and excrete, if your sense of thoroughness desires it—though, in fact, this wonderful un-body of yours can internally eliminate ingested food and fluid, which, of course, it does not depend on, without recourse to the accepted procedure. Any other mortal function is feasible. You can hiccup, sneeze, sweat, cry tears if the fancy takes you. You have a circulatory pseudo-blood system. You can even blush. But these rather fatuous demonstrations will not usually be triggered spontaneously. Not usually.

"There are a few restrictions that still apply. A few natural physical impulses that will relay so forcefully from your physical brain, that they'll govern your body haphazardly—fear, for example. Actually, I confess, I don't believe I've tracked them all down. You may get some surprises. The one sure biological law you'll still be subject to, however, is the sleep process. The human brain cannot perform effectively without some ration of sleep. The reasons for this are numerous, and I'll spare you them. In any event, physically you'll need little rest, and your sleep requirement will be appropriately low. You needn't worry about allocation. Lack will communicate itself. You'll get tired in the usual human manner, and lose consciousness in the same way. You'll be glad to hear your new body will continue to breathe and retain its other life signs during this time. Or maybe your thinking hasn't got far enough, yet, to see why realistic blood and comatose life signs are necessary.

"There's a second blatant stricture. Death. If you had any notions of escaping our friend, the Grim Reaper, you can erase those, too. Consciousness Transferral isn't a gate either to immortality or invulnerability. I don't know how long a human being can survive existence in a maintenance capsule. Experiments suggest indefinitely— after all, the wear and tear is slight and protection more or less infinite. Perhaps, on the other hand, atrophy will set in early despite the extreme ministrations of the mechanical nursemaid. If you take care of your capsule, I'd say you could expect at least thirty years of guaranteed life. But once your physical brain dies, your life is finished. Your consciousness goes out with it, and so, my Magdala, do you, whatever condition your simulate body is in. That is why I stress your care for the capsule. It's your ticket for the ride.

"Which leads me to death's appendix, injury. Don't

injure yourself, Magdala. I don't mean a broken ankle—though you're not completely unbreakable. I don't mean a grazed knuckle, either. Your wise new flesh mimics the mortal variety exactly. It can bleed and it can heal. But I don't mean any minor injury. What I do mean is, don't drown, don't walk under an auto-bus, don't jump from the roof of a building. Even your type of frame can't sustain that sort of treatment. In any case, the shock would kill you. Literally kill you. Because you can feel pain just as you can feel silk on your skin or sea-spray on your face. Your pseudo neurons are as efficient as the genuine ones. They'll send all their messages through your consciousness via your physical brain and back to your simulate, activating its response centers just like the originals. They have to, otherwise you couldn't see or hear, taste or feel or smell, or any of those things which you incredibly can do. But they'll let you have pain, as well, if the message that reaches your brain centers carries the correct pain cipher. Cut your finger, and you'll know it. So no crazy stunts. Excess pain can be a killer, even if it isn't happening to you at all."

There was a prolonged pause.

She heard the vibration of the tape fizzing from spool to spool. Then his voice came again. It was different. It had lost its clinically boastful note. It had become drunk with a clear white poison.

"You scared me," it said. "And what I've done. You still scare me. Perhaps I'll just drop by your capsule, and rip out the leads."

As the tape guttered into silence, Magdala's body sprang to its feet.

No longer alien, it was suddenly, essentially, her own. And her terror was pure, animal and overwhelming, uniting her forever with this flesh.

She hurled herself at the door and through it as it

opened. She raced, aware of the naked scintillance of her bare soles on the carpeted corridor, toward her small white room. Upright, light as a cat, beautiful, her body ran. This body *was* hers. She *knew* it. She loved it. If he cheated her, she would kill him—

Revelation came like a blow in the belly. She stopped running and sank to her knees at the entrance to the white room. She could almost catch his laughter, cruel and unstable, in the empty air.

She was looking straight at the capsule. Its leads were intact. It was all intact. If he had meant to do as he said, he would have done it hours ago, after he had finished recording his lecture. Done it as she postured before her mirrors, learning each glowing atom, each velvet nerve, each jeweled microcosm of skin. Or when she slept, an ultimate joke, he would have done it. No, he had offered even this threat with a purpose, electrically to charge her into unity and self-defense. And it had worked well. She had been electrified, and afraid. It was the first time fear had braced her since she had gazed into the mirror. She had not been afraid through all the afternoon, till now, Magdala Cled, Ugly, whose behavior had always been governed by the low inner throb of her fear. . . .

But fear persisted. She had deduced the subsidiary aspect of his game. She was intended to confront the capsule, as in the future she would have to. For, in this most uncanny fashion of all, she was going to have to learn to live with herself.

She had not yet grasped the full scope of his taped lesson; but enough. Ironically, she recognized that the inner chill that crept over her as she rose and advanced was the product of her brain within the capsule.

In the tilted glazium mummy-case, roped and entwined by apparatus and glimmering tubes, coroneted by its silver skull-cage, lay a gruesome crippled dwarf.

Magdala's gorge filled her throat, though she knew it did not, could not. (She could probably puke the food-digesting chemical bile if her distress sufficiently nauseated her, such was the strength of the stimuli from her brain. But it was simple to control, this second-hand mental impetus. While the anesthetized monster before her showed no sign of being the nausea's original fount.)

She stared at the monster. In revulsion. In a revulsion that could only be admitted now that she was liberated from hell.

And as she stared, superimposed upon the vile thing in its fantastic cradle, she beheld her glamor reflected in the glazium. Beauty and the Beast.

Magdala laughed. She had caught her inventor's madness.

It was a while before she registered that, apart from her two selves, and its own gadgets, the house was empty.

Night had evolved outside, smothering the salt beach. A golden rose of dawn had ascended inside, and lit up every chamber, passage, and vista. She had toyed with the toys of his house. Unclothed, she had enjoyed the naked sensation of silk and velvon, plastase or cool steel brushing her arms, legs, breasts, and shoulders. Sensuality was so fresh to her she had no name to give it.

She had penetrated to the kitchen area, thumbed switches, and perceived nut-brown toasts and strange sea food rising from hidden ovens to her plate. She ate, curious. She tasted every bite, chewed with strong white teeth, maneuvered with a strawberry tongue, swallowed, her creamy throat undulating. And then—the food seemed to lose itself somewhere in the region of her ribs, dissolve, vanish. It was like eliminex—but permanent; she had no hunger, though she had an appetite. She could digest perfectly, without a digestion.

At a touch, music soared and sank through the house.

Trivision flared. There was a Tri-V drama on the twelfth channel, it concerned a woman who would be classified as beautiful. The woman was not as beautiful as Magdala.

For the first time (all these first times), she knew the delight of vanity.

She had combed her blue-black hair, bathed her body slowly, slowly.

But she had done everything with a mounting sense, not yet realized, that Claudio was not there.

Finally, the awareness pierced through into her like a thin interminable noise in her ears. Alarm built quietly, layer on layer. When all layers were established, each atop the other, her fear fastened on her, her fear in a revised style.

Claudio was her mentor, her guardian. He was the magician. He was gone.

The reason for fear came eventually and revealed itself.

She was afraid to be alone, for alone, it seemed that none of this could be. It grew surrealistic. Without another to verify her condition, it might fade; a blown-out fire, a mirage.

She retreated, room by room, till she reached the room with the five walls. She turned on the mirrors and sat in the middle of them, glancing from each to each. And the mirrors seemed to exclaim: *Here you are. See! You exist.*

This phase lasted a long time.

At length, she heard the striking electro-battery clock which she had switched on in one of the chambers beneath. It struck twenty-five tones. Each tone thrilled through the house, a brazen tuning-fork. It was midnight.

Magdala got up. The syndrome of disbelief fell away, and she was abruptly conscious of her nudity. Before, the body had been a garment in itself.

He had deserted her in the computerized house,

without preparation and without clothes. At last, with an acid and reassuring anger, she had analyzed her predicament as another test. Possibly he was not even absent from the house, but spying from some wily camouflage. Gauging her.

She could move fluidly now, delectably.

I am delectable.

Let him judge her, then. She was not a machine, not a robot. (Did she know what she was? She was his creation.) She stabbed the remaining buttons on the panel by the door, to see what else the mirror room would bring her.

The ultimate button brought her a gray cottene bath robe.

A pang of rage shot through her. He was playing with her again. Disappointing her. She put the robe on and tied it. She had expected silk. She was beginning to think as her body suited her to think. Her aspirations, in this short space, were already being tailored by her flesh: The delectable woman could anticipate delectable adornment. Maybe it was not so new. It was what society had conditioned her to anticipate. (The girls and young men from the processory, shedding their overalls, stepping forth like peacocks into the sunlight of the city.)

Below her, in the house, she heard someone whistling. Next the sound of ice in crystal, clear as bells through the pool of silence.

She let the ramp carry her down, then jumped, utterly coordinated, lightly and exquisitely into the room.

The sunrise light had dimmed smokily, but did not unduly limit vision.

The man in the pneumatic chair was not the man she had reckoned on. It was not Claudio. Though the iced beaker, a rich man's foible, not glazium but wafer-thin glass, that was Claudio's, and it chimed lethargically, familiarly, in the man's hand as he kissed it to his lips.

III

HIS HAIR WAS BLACK, but a black inclined to red rather than blue. Reddish-brown eyes confirmed the bias. His skin was deeply tanned from a solarium, and the pressure-zipped jacket and trousers were expensive. Another rich man.

Her immediate inclination was to run to the white room above, where the capsule lay, bald and vulnerable. She resisted that, confronted by his posture of somehow irreversibly seated indolence. For a moment, then, she was Ugly. Her body bowed, leaned into a crouch, trying to shield, to efface. But it did not persist, this spasm. She remembered what she was. Every shiny surface in the room was there to assist in reminding her.

"Who are you?" she said. "How did you get in?" She had been lucky in that. In the Tri-V drama she had briefly watched earlier, the woman had come on an intruder in her apartment. "Who are you?" she had rasped. "How did you get in?" Magdala's imitation was excellent.

"I am a friend," the man said. He was letting his russet eyes slip down the length of her. "I guess you are also a—friend. How do friends get in? They knock and the door is opened."

His scrutiny failed to cause a second trauma. Instead, she basked in it, recalling vividly what he would see. And the recollection, coupled with his long-lidded gaze, excited her. A sentence suggested itself. Again, she had heard other women employ it.

"It seems I interest you."

Her head moved, stirring the blue hair like ink in water. It was becoming intuitive.

"Yes," he said, "you do. You're really something."

She accepted the stale accolade. She was not aware that she nodded in agreement. But the man laughed a little. He said: "Where do you come from? What's your name?"

Suddenly, she saw no need to render him anything beyond the sumptuous image of herself, powered with the smoky light. "You should ask Claudio."

"But Claudio's not here for the moment."

"Oh, I think he's here somewhere. But if you're a friend of his, no doubt you're used to the games he likes to play."

"You tell me," the stranger drawled, "about his games. What games does he play with you, for example? I'd be fascinated."

For a second she was afraid. Sex was an unknown country, and this verbal exchange along its borders seemed all at once dangerous and unpleasant. At the same moment, she knew herself aroused, and a silly humorousness added itself to the medley of her emotions, that she had been equipped, even for this.

Her heart was speeding, not because it had to, but presumably because her mood induced it to act in complementary physical rhythm. She wondered how near Claudio was, and if he spied on this, too. She wondered if he might be affected as she was becoming affected.

The man was attractive. She could likely seduce him, as the women in the Tri-V dramas generally did with men. Or the men with the women. Indigo was a world of untrammeled lust, from which, she had been trained from childhood to realize, she was excluded. But now, no longer excluded. Now she was Venus, goddess of love.

"Games interest you, do they?" She let herself topple in an appalled delirium. "Let's play one."

And as she said it, she noticed that the man cast no shadow, and that where his arms rested along the arms of the chair, the form-cushioning plastase had not altered its shape.

The wild scared heat in her throat and groin went cold. Cold froze her eyes and mouth. She had stumbled, as she always stumbled, into yet another of Claudio's traps. She could not make her voice come for half a minute. Then she got it out, hard and jagged.

"When the leaves fall from the trees outside, they disappear. A millionaire's holostetic forest, turned on or off by a switch or a button. How much did the man cost to design and project, Claudio? Is he sufficiently realistic that he can put his arms around me? Or will I need a sensit headset for that?"

The man winked out like a lamp; even the glass disappeared. Claudio walked from a wall, clapping.

"Good," he said. *"Good."*

She averted her face, but he came and stood over her.

"Holostets have their limitations," he said. "The trees are fine. They work strictly to a pre-program, without variety. But a holostet that seems to react must be controlled, and from a distance of not more than ten meters. And to get the damned thing to talk calls for feats you would scarcely credit. But you. You work very nicely on your own, don't you? Quite a display. You must take after your mother, Mary of Magdala. A thoroughbred whore."

The oddly anachronistic gibe struck her as ludicrous.

She glanced up and met his eyes, and the tide within her changed direction, though Tri-V still ordered her vocal chords. She had remembered how she had envisaged him, the voyeur, spying on her own arousal; the choice of words he had given the holostet illusion.

"Well," she said, "you've paid my price already." And waited, her body emotively unbreathing, for his reply.

"Me?" he smiled, wide-eyed. "My apologies, Magdala. I assure you it was just a test-run on your unconsidered retaliation to an event. Preparation for the world outside. Nothing else. You forget, I know what you actually look like. No thanks."

She shriveled. And, even as she shrank from him, she smelled his cruelty, pungent as burning wires. It was another first. For the first time, she was attempting to investigate the motives of those who wounded her.

"Don't cry over it," he said. "You shouldn't find tears easy, as you are. You'll need to practice that, too." But she had not cried in sixteen years. She was a desert, and in her desert she had the leisure to begin to hate him, an efficient chiseled hatred, new to her as everything.

The sunrise fitting spilled in his blond hair and down his well-dressed, slim, young-man's body. His beauty was like a razor's edge.

Even now that he had made her equally beautiful, it could comfort her to hate Claudio Loro.

"I suggest you go back to your room," he said. "Go and sit with the mirrors."

He had dropped the silver discs into his ears.

She went.

She read from the electrobook screen through the remainder of the night. The library was vast. She spun the dial at random, and read random sections, spinning the dial again if she grew uninterested, or if the tumult of her thoughts intruded; also to mislead him, for he was probably keeping track of everything she did.

The window wall faced north across the bay. The sun rose on the right side of the house, and the sky and the agitated waves lightened, distracting her. There was a mist, and through it the sea resembled blue milk.

When she turned back to the electrobook screen, the page had melted, and a trivisual image of Claudio was there instead.

Charmingly, and extraneously, he informed her:

"I'm afraid you can't keep me out. The house does exactly as I tell it. You have no privacy. However, I thought you should know. The enchanting dummy-run last night, with our holostet visitor, wasn't pointless. In a couple of days' time, we're traveling a hundred kilometers down the coast together, into the thick of a crowd. I'm curious to observe how you cope. I don't offer you a choice, by the way. You're obliged to come with me."

There was a silence.

"Yes," she said. She was trembling, but the trembling was metaphysical and had not reached her body. Somehow, she was able to prevent its doing so.

"I'll discuss details with you later," he said.

His image darkened, and the page of the book she had been reading replaced it.

The new ache of her hatred did not interfere with her obedience.

Hating, she sat and read his books.

Three

The Proving-Ground

I

THERE WAS STILL summer grass at Sugar Beach, though it was blueing. Just a faint sheen as yet on the edges of hills that sloped down like baked ginger biscuit in the dusk to the sky-color talcum of the sand. Sand which sloped a farther four hundred meters to the sky-color rollers of the sea.

Between the hills and the beach rested the hotel complex, its flashing glazium windows beginning to turn their blank, one-way gold eyes upon the ocean, its three stabilized and incorruptible piers stretched out into the water. The transparent revolving restaurant that was its centerpiece, had started the evening carousel.

Five hundred cars were drawn up in the subground park. Fifty more allegedly lay in the private garages of particular guests, accessible from the individual apartments above. There was specific space for seven hundred vehicles. Every sunset the cars poured into the hotel. They sped from the research plants, laboratories, fish farms, and experimental stations that lay within the vicinity, the eight hundred and forty-two kilometers that constituted the coastal strip and sporadic inland salt basin of Sapphire Flats. There were other resorts, but

Sugar Beach was Sugar Beach, if you could afford it.
Near dawn, most of the cars poured out again, as the
tide poured out from the shore.

The roof of the revolving restaurant had been peeled
open in segments like those of a grapefruit. Light balled
upward, wiping out the stars.

In its gold-work jail, a casino balanced between floor
and sky. The first bouts of the night were commencing,
Soleil Noir, Baccarat, and Spin. Below, the circular ring
of tables descended in tiers to the orchestrated funnel of
a dancing area where a tri-visual sea, photo-refracted up
from receptors sunk in the banks of the hotel piers, con-
vincingly swirled, alive with fish, about the slowly syn-
copating couples. The current dance was the Cling,
which supplied three basic steps and the pressure of
torso on torso. It was the dance of a society that used its
energy and intellect in other ways, a dance of relaxation,
the discreet prelude to sex.

There was not a defective face in the enormous room,
and no slack bodies. De-calorized foods and calisthenic
machinery abetted persons already bred initially by
mathematical selection, gene with gene. Yet the univer-
sality of pleasing features produced an oddly flavorless
effect, only here and there relieved by those whose pre-
conceptional selection match had resulted in some high
point of attraction. It was, however, apparent that selection very rarely gave rise to sheer beauty. Beauty, it
seemed, like ugliness, was normally an accident, something unplanned, the biological collision of chromo-
somes.

Heads were certainly turning as the man and the
woman walked down the tiers toward their table. But if
their looks might be one cause, the second had to be
their obvious wealth.

To be rich was not unheard of. But to be as rich as this
was eye-catching. Astrads subtly sang around them like

heat on the air. Foremost, the fabric of their garments: off-planet imported materials. There was a silk stripe in the blond man's white evening clothes, his shoes were white leather with toe-caps of durascened flexium silver. And silver links fastened the front of the violet shirt together, replacing the ubiquitous invisible pressure-zip. On the man's left wrist was a heavy copper timepiece, antique and probably handcrafted. For her part, the black-haired woman seemed to have been dipped into a black and starry night, into the starry night of space itself. The dress described her body, made love to it, and the stars were phosphor diamonds. She had no additional jewelry, apart from her nails, each of which was capped with thin, shaped amber. Neither man nor woman wore cosmetics, and neither needed to. Their faces were smooth with the indefinable maquillage of introspection.

One of Sugar Beach's uniformed attendants ushered them into their seats. Three waiters approached.

A lamp above the table dissolved languorously from rose to purple, purple to blue, blue to green to yellow to rose. Bathed in its ichors, the duet chose their meal and wine was ordered. The man seemed indolently in command, the woman sublimely quiescent.

Two pale emerald bottles of archaic glass were brought to the table, covered with frost.

Covertly, the tiered ring watched. Dancers coming up or descending to the fishy tunnel of the tri-visual sea dance floor, glanced with swift impaling glances. The gamblers in their golden cage above now and then glanced down between the crack of spins, the whir of the wheel, the dry slap of plastic cards, and the drier rattle of plastic chips.

"You're doing well," Claudio said, as they drank the ice-green wine. His unremitting scrutiny was like a scalpel.

It dissected everything she did, each movement, each breath she took. Tension held her rigid, but the rigidity did not infect her bodily articulation. She could do all things fluently, while her mind shook and her instincts calcified. Casually, deliberating, as if watching mercury rise or fall, he asked her: "How do you feel?"

"How do you suppose I feel?"

He seemed to like and not to like her knack of handling language sparely and deflectively, an ability which became more pronounced with use.

"You're frightened," he said. "Naturally. Home in that encapsulated brain of yours, among your tangle of wires and valves and pretty lights. That's where your fear is. It doesn't show here, but here you feel it."

Her antipathy to him had improved her poise. Obedience to him removed the vacillation that might undermine the effect of this poise. She was turning in a finished performance. It did not perplex him, but plainly it affected him in some oblique way.

"Your reactions interest me. Especially when you strive to check them," he said, with a dangerous placidity.

Their food came, and she ate. It was simple for her body to swallow and eradicate the food, even though her throat seemed locked. She had only to let the body act out its clever role. She could rely on that. There were hundreds of other eyes upon her, eyes which were not Claudio's. These eyes were terrifying. The myriad looks, stares, gazes drenched her, and she had been afraid she might forget, believe herself once more Ugly, crouched in the darkest booth of the Accomat Cafeteria. But she did not forget, not now. The lovely hands with their jewelry nails were there to reassure her, and the space-fabric frock, curled about her feet, and her silk hair brushing her cheeks and neck.

And the hundreds of eyes which had fastened on her could reassure her too. They were mirrors, blind as mirrors. None of them knew her secret, knew where it lay, the hideous dwarf in its glazium box. Only Claudio knew. Only Claudio was careful to remind her.

He had ordered four courses. As the second was cleared by one of the uniformed waiters, a couple, man and girl, approached the table.

Magdala stared back at them, and panic began to pour through into her. It never reached her face. At the exact summit of this peak of her, she saw, unalleviated, her effect upon the human race.

The girl had hair the soft red of synthetic fire, and she went directly to Claudio, as if to some lost object she had been continually searching for.

Magdala had drearily envied others their normalcy. To regret the unobtainable was irresistible. But more than envy, she had hated them. Now, surprising her, there was still an impulse to hate.

"Claudio," stated the girl. He rose, and she placed her hands lightly on his shoulders. "Where have you been all summer? Why did you never call me?"

"I think I see why," said her companion, the man.

"My sister," Claudio said. "Magda, make yourself gregarious."

The man took Magdala's hand and kissed her palm.

"My God, you're beautiful," he said. His eyes waited for her response. How could he know she had learned?

"Am I?" she said.

"Sister, did he say?" the man asked.

"If he says so."

Claudio turned to Magdala and the girl said, cutting across him: "Well, well. Kith and kin."

Blond Claudio, clad in a white suit, his eyes yellowish metal tinged by verdigris, indicated the woman with her blue-black hair, blue eyes, star-dusted black gown and freckle-dusted luminous skin. "Don't you see the family resemblance?"

"Now that you mention it," the man said, "maybe I can. I'm Irlin. Do you do the Cling, Magda?"

"I don't dance."

"Claudio does," said the girl. "Come on, dance me, Claudio."

"Why not?" said Claudio.

He went away with the girl, down the steps, into the sea funnel. Magdala watched them begin to move together. Their bodies suitably clung, and the three steps came and went with a fluid carelessness. Tri-V fish swam between them and the other dancers. The red-haired girl stretched to meet Claudio, mouth to mouth. The sea covered them, they disappeared.

"I guess I've lost my partner," said Irlin. "Are you sure you don't dance?"

"No."

He edited his hand over hers.

"You know what they say. If you dance on a floor, you can do the same in bed."

She looked at his hand on hers.

If you found out what you were touching, Irlin.

"Is he really your brother?" said Irlin, caressing her hand.

"Of course. If he says so."

"Oh. You want me to leave you alone?"

"No. I want you to tell me about Claudio."

Irlin blinked, and called her bluff.

"You're kidding. Surely you know your own brother."

Magdala drew her hand aside, opened her purse, and took out an identity card. She displayed it. The name on the card was Magda Loro.

"We're seldom together," said Magdala. She was still using Tri-V dialogue, since the apposite celluloid phrases somehow could elicit replies. "I like to hear about him. He's reticent. I expect you noticed."

"I've only met him twice," said Irlin. "The girl I'm with, Nada, she and Claudio had a couple of nights before the summer. But he's a blank screen to me. A rich man—he doesn't work, he hasn't any fads or ties. Lily-of-the-field astrad-types; butterflies. And you're the same. What do you do on the planet?"

"I live," she said.

"Christ. I've seen. Sorry, forget it. What I mean is, I'm staying at Sugar, six and sevenday of this Dek. Come swimming."

"I don't swim."

"You know what they say," repeated Irlin dogmatically. "Still, maybe you don't do that, either. I could teach you," said Irlin.

"To swim."

"Anything. Anything you'd like to learn. You really are beautiful."

Magdala turned to him and tried to see him. He looked like everyone else. Attractive, ordinary, healthy. The picture wouldn't gel, and she realized she would forget the instant he was gone. Over his broad shoulder, she saw Claudio returning from the sea funnel, the girl Nada ahead of him. Her lids were wet and her face, under its pearly powder, white. She stalked to the table.

"Leave it," said Nada to Irlin.

Irlin seemed irritated. His eyes lingered on Magdala, but Nada seized his arms. "Leave it, I said. Or stay, and I'll call an autocab back to the plant."

"Excuse me," said Irlin, and followed Nada away.

Claudio sat down, and the three waiters came at once with the third course of their meal.

"Was it fun?" Claudio asked.

"You should have watched."

"I had other business."

"They don't know," said Magdala, "that you are a scientist."

"They aren't intended to. Money can buy obscurity as well as a false I.D. for one's friends."

"I showed the false I.D. to Irlin. He didn't believe I was your sister."

"You astound me."

"He wants to take me swimming."

"He wants to fuck you. Interested?"

"What did you say to that girl?" Magdala started to eat. Her fear had already died, and a curious depression was smothering her. Fragments of the books she had read flowed about her mind. She wished she were alone, hidden, asleep.

"I told her she was tedious. She is. She was. Only you are not tedious, my Magdala. You are appallingly, horribly untedious."

Shrieks came from the gold gambling jail above. Someone was winning. Or had lost.

Claudio's suite at Sugar Beach had five rooms and two bathrooms. It was decorated in beige, gold, and blue and cost five hundred and thirty astrads a day. An elevator, exclusive to the suite, negotiated the thirty floors into the private subground garage pertaining to the suite. Here the great silver car lay beneath a transparent dust-shield. Built into the under-chassis of the car was a secondary storage compartment, excavated on the left-hand side by a concealed corridor, two meters in length, one and a half meters in circumference.

You got into the elevator and dropped down the thirty floors. You raised the dust-shield. In the flank of the car, a panel (similarly concealed) could be opened, a button pressed. In the under-chassis, the otherwise indiscernible corridor was gradually revealed. A second button, and the corridor's burden emerged: the stabilized glazium mummy-case, with its contents.

"Have you read any Grotesque Fiction? The Vampire?" Claudio had said. "He could travel nowhere without his coffin. Not only do you have a traveling coffin, Magdala, you have a body to go with it."

He had showed her the storage space and how the cylinder fitted inside, about the same time he showed her the clothes he had purchased for her from exclusive city stores, and the bizarre forgery of the I.D. card. Her photo-fix was on the card and the name he had evolved for her, plus her index and thumb prints—no longer, actually, her own, but the body's prints, alien. She did not ask how he had arranged the I.D.—if his wealth could merely buy E.C. government bureaucracy on Indigo, or if his flamboyant skills had created the card. She asked always little of Claudio. He schooled her in what to wear, what to do, and now and then in what to say. He did not school her in the gallery of insecurities and mistrusts which clouded her thoughts. He did not teach her how to stave off madness.

She believed he was mad, after all. Her own lapse into hysteria must follow inevitably. It was all an insanity. Why not?

At five in the morning, she took the elevator and plunged into the ground. Stepping out into the garage area, she raised the dust-shield of the car, worked the panel and the buttons, and at length stood beside herself.

Sleep was barely necessary, but sleep would have enabled her to escape. Claudio was gone—to gamble in the all-night casino or to the room of one of the several women who had presented themselves to him throughout the evening. There had been other men, too, for Magdala, other Irlins, good-looking, mediocre, and unmemorable. The holostet, for some reason, had had more presence for her than these living men. She could remember the holostet, the red-black hair and red-brown eyes.

She visualized, childishly, the fur cat lying waiting for her in the shut-couch at the Accomat. Her new thumb would no longer activate the lock of her apartment.

She forced herself to look into the putty face inside the glazium, wreathed with its wires and its bright head-piece.

The coffin.

II

AT TEN O'CLOCK in the morning, Irlin called.
"It's a wonderful sunny Blue day. The flowers by
the pool are turning blue. Not as blue as your eyes,
Magda."

They regarded each other through the medium of the
Call-vision-plates. The apartment behind him was not
as large as any of the five chambers of Claudio's suite.
Irlin had remained unmemorable.

Uneasily he said, "Your brother was with Nada last
night. Maybe we were both lonely, you and me. Can I
meet you at the pool?"

"I don't think so."

He was the first of four calls from strangers.

At thirteen, Claudio entered the suite with Nada.

Nada wore a scarlet dress, and the air seemed to
catch alight, as she passed through, from her chemical
redness. They crossed into one of the bathrooms, and
the door shut. A shower was switched on, and female
laughter emanated.

Half an hour afterward, Claudio walked through
Magdala's bedroom door. He had changed his clothes,

and his undried hair was dark from the shower, which she could still hear distantly plashing.

"Why didn't you invite Irlin up?" said Claudio. "The suite would relax him after the candy jar he's paying to stay in. But you'll see him at lunch. You can arrange it then."

"Arrange what?" she said. Her voice sounded listless. She stared from the window across the blue beach to the blue sea. Both blues were spasmodically alive with animated forms.

"I've seen what's happening to you," he said sharply. "It's the second stage. First elation, then withdrawal. Such things are predictable. But you're coming down to eat a meal and display yourself, whether you want to or not. You're going to go on with this till I tell you it's finished. Irlin is optional, though I imagine your Magadalene itch will guide you unerringly in that direction. You are fully constructed, Magda. To the last detail."

Magdala turned slowly and looked at him.

She held out her right hand, palm open, fingers spread.

"Constructed of what?"

"Oh, God. We don't have to discuss this now. The redhead's in the shower."

"I feel of skin and muscle. My mouth has moisture, and my eyes. My hair feels like hair."

"*Not now.*"

"Now!" she said, but she found the cinnamon voice was screaming. "Now! Now!"

He caught her hand. He twisted and gripped the hand and it hurt her. This body, which could be hurt, was her own, was hers. This was all she was. She had dreamed the thing in the capsule.

"Grown skin and grown hair," he rapped out at her. "Cellular growth after a blueprint in a growth tank, inner organs built like machine parts inside a machine. Put together like a doll. You're a clock, Magda. Vellum outside and tick-tock inside. Tick Magdala. Tick tock. You can do it all, Magdala. You can even screw. But don't foul it up for me."

"What?" she said.

He smiled, twisting her hand into a knot of white-hot pain.

"My experiment. My Deus ex machina. My Frankenstein. Don't foul it, monster."

He let her free exactly as the door opened. The redhead burned through like a thin intense fire which closed doors could not deny.

"Are we going down, Claudio?"

"Call Irlin to join us. Table fifteen on Pier Three."

"*Irlin?*" the girl snapped.

"Do it."

She walked out and pushed buttons on the Call.

"Are you ready?" Claudio asked Magdala.

"Yes."

"When she's settled Irlin, you and Nada will go down together, do you understand? I'll follow you."

She moved by him, not answering, her eyes unfocused. He snatched her hair, holding her a second. "Just," he said, "get it right."

In the descending elevator, Nada unnecessarily repearlized her face before a compact mirror, and did not utter. Irlin stood waiting for the two women at the edge of the beach.

The end of Pier Three spread into a wide railed platform. One of the thermostatic hotel pools, its water colored a mild yellow, opened in the center and flowed under the translucent plexiglaze floor. A poppy-red canopy flapped above the tables in the warm sea wind.

Claudio had placed the silver music discs in his ears. It was like eating lunch with a deaf man. Sometimes he smiled at them with absent-minded courteous rudeness. He heard nothing, yet seemed to miss nothing either.

Frustrated, the red girl grew sullen beneath the red canopy, and dumb to rival Claudio's deafness. Irlin was clearly embarrassed. He broke into wisecracks which slumped leadenly dead.

They had a lot to drink with lunch, frothy aperitifs and several long glasses of spirits with the meal.

Magdala uninterestedly swallowed these liquids, for the drink could not work upon her new system, only on her palate; she was incapable of intoxication. Then, quite suddenly, she was floating.

The disoriented buoyancy horrified her. She had never been drunk in her life, her actual life. She had believed she could not now become drunk. It did not make sense—

She looked at Claudio.

"Irlin," he said, through the music playing in his head, "my sister is thawing under the influence of lunch. Take her fishing."

Magdala's fear was trying to secure her attention, but the euphoric separation the alcohol had produced shut off her fear from her. She groped after the acrid savor of it.

Irlin grinned foolishly.

"Fishing?"

"I can't hear you," said Claudio.

"Would you like to go fishing?" Irlin asked Magdala. Her voice would not come. She nodded, frowning.

She did not understand. She did not care that she did not understand.

Irlin took her arm, and they left the table and walked back along the pier. Near the shore, a concrete apron extended westward. Here men and women sat with steel rods and treated gut lines, enjoying a barbaric pastime, the sun on their backs. There was rarely a catch. The eternal motion and noise on the three piers warned off the fish, along with the shadows thrown ink-blue into the water.

Magdala leaned on the rail above the apron. Her hair fanned and pleated in the warm wind. She could feel her own beauty, her slenderness, her own curves pressed into the rail. She closed her eyes, stunned by what she beheld in her mind of her manifested self.

"Magda," said Irlin huskily. He fondled her shoulder; his hand pleased her, stroking her moodily, symmetrically, in tune with the peculiar tides that were running through her. "I wish I was rich. Again, I wish I was rich. Are you a beautiful snob, Magda?" She could hear, dimly, that he was a little drunk too. "Butterfly," he said, "light on me, butterfly. Beautiful, freckled butterfly."

There was a scuffle, a cry. Magdala raised her lids.

"Someone's got a fish," Irlin said distractedly.

It was a fact. Reeling in frantically, two men jerked up the gut from the ocean, and the fish was dragged after to land violently on the apron. It was a double-tailed cody, the edible variety. Sea-bright, blue-silver, it flung itself along the concrete. White blood splattered from its mouth around the hook. The crowd on the apron laughed and shouted as they waited for it to die.

Magdala turned quickly away, her back now to the rail.

Across the width of the pier, twelve meters from her, a man had halted, looking at her.

She identified him. The red-black hair, the tanned skin. The holostetic man Claudio had tricked her with.

But it could not be a holostet. Not here. Instinctively, her eyes sought for a shadow at his feet, and found it. He wore a white zip top and fawn trousers. A thick silver wristlet on his left arm snagged the sun into her eyes. He was real.

He came toward her and stopped half a meter away.

"What are you doing here?" he said flatly.

Magdala said nothing.

Irlin stirred at her side.

"Who's this, Magda?"

The man showed his flawless teeth.

"Oh, Magda, is it? Well, *Magda*, you know who it is, don't you?"

"No," she said.

"Don't you, Magda? But I saw you recognize me," the man said innocently. It was nightmarishly apt. "Anyway, can I assume it was you sent me the stelex to meet you here?"

She gazed at him, and the pier seemed sliding from beneath her. She was drunk, and the man before her was the figment of some hallucination, except that Irlin saw him too.

"Take a walk on the water," Irlin now said. "The lady doesn't know you."

The man reached out and patted Magdala's cheek.

"You're cut, aren't you?" said the man. "We'll settle it when you've sobered up. What's your room number?"

Irlin hit him. It was a tutored, text-book blow, infallible though sloppy in delivery. The man dropped at their feet.

"Christ," said Irlin. He stumbled up the pier, pulling Magdala beside him.

III

IRLIN ASKED no questions. Yet he was nervous. He seemed to believe the second rich man who had accosted them on the pier was some ghost from her rich-girl's past.

Nobody else approached. Public arguments and fights would be part of the entertainment at Sugar Beach, to be taken in from a safe spectator's vantage.

"Where now?" Irlin said.

Recklessly, she said: "Not the hotel. Get your car and drive me somewhere."

"Where?"

"Surprise me."

She was becoming inventive with the Tri-V dialogue, and her drunkenness was delicious. What did it matter about the black-haired man?

Irlin led her to a small slick car. They climbed inside. He activated the robot-drive and punched in the program buttons. When the car started up, he slouched unrelaxedly, and watched the shooting gray ribbon of road erupt before the windscreen.

She was exhilarated by the speed. It seemed to complement the alcoholic high. Leaving Claudio's silver

house, she had seen him switch off the holoset trees
inside the wall. One moment they existed, then they did
not. Her fear was like that. Her fear, which had seemed
so palpable, had been switched off.

They drove into the blued-over, gingerbread hills, to
an isolated run-down bar, and sat on the glazium veranda, drinking synthetic wine. She did not get any
drunker, but the momentum did not lapse.

Not many people came to this cheap bar. Another
couple had gone up into a room. The air-wash was
faulty, and the reversible windows open. Presently Magdala heard the girl noisily producing an orgasm.

Alone with her on the veranda, Irlin's nervousness
seemed to increase his concern to touch her. He ran his
hand over her shoulder, along the inside of her arm
against her breast. She turned to him and allowed him
to kiss her. The kiss was like the blow—tutored, calcu-
lated, effective, and unclever.

"Don't be plastic," he said into her mouth. "Come
with me, baby, come with me."

His hand went on moving down and down the slopes
of her. His fingers wadded aside her skirt, kneaded the
unclothed skin of her thigh.

"You're so lovely," he said.

As suddenly as it had swamped her, as if at signal, her
drunkenness ebbed away. She tried to keep it from leaving her, but without success. She sank after it. The blue
on the hills became dismal, the day sodden with heat,
his hand damp and insistent and no longer compatible.

She was afraid. Alone with a stranger, and afraid.

She was ugly, crippled, deformed, and a young man
was rubbing his hands all over her and sighing in her ear.

She pushed at him.

"No more."

"Please, Magda—"

"No."

He complied, shivering.

She rose, and picked her way off the veranda, toward the car-park. Soon he followed her, hanging his head, his eyes raw with a loathing he could not or would not express.

"You do it with your brother," he managed eventually, and opened the car for her. They drove back to the hotel.

The sun was burning the western sky and the crenellated tips of the sea. She fidgeted in Irlin's car, watching the sun. There was no sign of the black-haired man.

"What I said," Irlin muttered. He stared at her, the loathing in his eyes, troubled by propriety, "I made a mistake."

"Never mind," she said foolishly.

She got out of the car and ran into the hotel, and into the elevator which bore her upwards. When the door of the suite widened she experienced an almost immediate relief. Then she saw Claudio.

He sat facing the door. He was serene, immaculate.

"Poor Irlin," he said. "The lady hadn't thawed after all."

Abruptly, her descent from the alcoholic high was complete, and with a wretched rationality she understood.

"I couldn't be drunk," she said. "The neurons can relay stimuli by proxy from my brain and into it, to trigger neural circuits, but drink is different. It's like food—taste, scent, texture only. Unless my *physical* body were drunk. Then I'd feel it—wouldn't I?" She waited, straight and stony, challenging him. "What did you do?"

"A little spirit distilled through the feed-drip in your maintenance capsule. Harmless. Arranged to coincide with the progress of your own pseudo-drinking. I did it when you and the redhead went down to the pier."

"Why?"

"As always. To manipulate you and revel in the enchanting result."

No turmoil began in her. She was aware of a great alteration in herself. She was aware of anger, like an unlit fuse, anger and hate and power, all in abeyance. In herself, she was stilled.

"There was a man on the pier," she said. "He apparently knew me."

"A familiar gambit."

"He was the original of the holostet man you used in the house."

Claudio's eyes and mouth widened into childlike shock. He flung out his arms stiffly, hands upheld in incredulity like a puppet. The deliberate overacting was frankly intended to negate her.

She went by him, into her bedroom, into the bathroom and turned on the shower. She stripped and offered herself to the stinging spray, tepid, then hot, then cool.

She sensed him leaning by the bedroom door.

Presently he said: "His name is Paul Hovak. He's ostensibly on E.C. government payroll, a coordinator for twenty or so subsidiary chemical research projects on Indigo. He's wealthy, mostly anonymous, and almost certainly has political affiliations outside E.C. He has learned a lot of jargon about the basics of subchem, and a lot more about wheels within wheels and strings that work strings—which the luckless hard-hitting Irlin will discover when he's fired next oneday."

She did not reply. She listened to the shower, rinsing her body, not thinking. She was still switched off, like the electric trees of Claudio's holostet forest.

She sensed Claudio shift beside the door.

"When you dress, put on the present I've left you."

She sensed him go away. She sensed the suite empty of him as if of its air.

Through the vacuum, she stepped from the shower into the drier.

In the bedroom, the dress hung ready, released from

its plastase dust-resister: auburn satin with a coal-blue fringe of crystals across the shoulders. The matched coal crystal nails rose like thorns from their box, and beside them, a three-chain bracelet of black sapphires.

Without thinking or considering, she had become fully alert. She lifted the bracelet, and ran her thumb along it. The telltale vibration was in the middle clasp. A micro-recorder, three hours' worth of miniaturized tape, already active.

She dressed and fastened the bracelet on her arm. Obediently.

She was not wondering about anything.

She was still switched off, like the electric trees.

When the switch re-engaged, what would happen?

She selected a perfume sachet, and squeezed its liquor into her palm. To the fragrance of Earthindian Sandalwood, like an accompaniment, the door buzzed.

Not Claudio. Claudio and she possessed the plastic insert tags which unlocked the door from outside. Perhaps Nada, or Irlin. But she comprehended who it was.

She would not answer, then.

On her arm, the recorder in the bracelet—faintly, faintly.

Yes, she was meant to answer.

She opened the door, and the black-haired man stood there. Paul Hovak.

"Let me in," Paul Hovak said. So she let him in.

He strolled deep into the room.

"Pleasing," he said. "Of course, your salary is adequate. Or is someone keeping you?"

"Someone is keeping me," she said.

"Then I trust he's away right now."

And briskly he went to every door of the suite, opening them, glancing inside, even into the two bathrooms.

She remembered the conversation in the silver house, when she had supposed she spoke to this man and did not. His real voice, his real attitude, were quite unlike those of the holostet. The actual Paul Hovak was crisp in his approach. He had not referred to the scene on the pier. His bruised jaw had been salved and showed no mark of its injury. Satisfied they were alone, he now seated himself. His demeanor conveyed the impression that all former business had been an error he had eradicated, and they could begin again, on this occasion operating efficiently.

In perfect unenlightenment, scenting both the sinister and the makeshift in this charade, Magdala said, Tri-V style:

"Will you have a drink?"

"No, I don't think so. I don't think you will either. Let's get to the point. You sent me an innuendo-packed stelex, unsigned. I was to meet you. I am here. What's the news?"

Claudio, the magician. He had sent the stelex to this man. He had formed the holostet in this man's likeness in order that she exhibit a show of recognition. Claudio was manipulating both of them. Evidently, the man's assumptions were intended to shatter on her own ignorance of the situation. (The deduction was casual.) Possibly, having been informed of the man's name, she was meant to use it.

"M. Hovak—or do I say Paul," she said. "What news?"

"I'm tired of this," Hovak said. "I haven't the space to waste my time. Do you have anything, or not?"

"I would say . . . not."

His face coalesced and darkened. There was sweat on his forehead and upper lip.

He said, "What's the matter with you?" He left a lacuna for her interjection. When none came, he said, "All right. I'll assume this is just an exercise in insecurity on your part. You're making sure I'll be prompt when you do have results. When do you go back?"

"Back to where?"

"To Marine Bleu. Where the hell else?"

"Is that where I'm going?"

He rose and strode across the room to her. As he loomed, the switch clicked on inside her. She reverted to absolute terror as his hard, real-life hands clamped down on her shoulders and his dry hot breath scoured her face.

"I'm not in the market for clowning," he said. His voice stayed crisp as his fingers gouged the fringes into her arms. "Don't clown, Christa. Just get the goods you promised. The goods you're taking such a goddam long time over delivering. Hear me? The very next call I have from you is going to be *The* Call. Yes?"

She had to stop him.

"Yes," she said, "whatever you say."

He let her flesh and dress out of his grasp. He and she fell away from each other, breathing thickly.

Paul Hovak shook his head as if he had emerged from water.

"Your nerves are in a bad way," he said. "That's a warning. Don't crack up on me. I want this thing, and I'm betting on you, Christa." He walked to the door. "I'll be leaving in half an hour. When did you say you're due back at Marine Bleu?"

She closed her hand over the three chains of the bracelet.

"Three days."

"O.K. Get some rest. And lay off the syrup."

The door slid sideways and he went through it and along the corridor.

Whatever Claudio had wished for had presumably been accomplished, and was audibly captured on the tape in her bracelet. The sapphires glowed warm under her fingers. With a wooden thoroughness, Magdala unsnapped the triple clasp, and as she did so, her passivity faded.

IV

SHE MADE CERTAIN of Hovak's departure at the foyer desk registration screen, then took the moving stair and stepped out into the great gold casino suspended high above the restaurant.

"May I buy chips against my brother's account?"

"Yes, M. Loro. Of course."

They brought her one thousand white chips in a scoop.

Below, she could not see Claudio's platinum head, though her scan of the tiers was brief. Down in the sea funnel, the tunes which radiated from the speakers were different, but couples were still dancing the Cling. Overhead, through the peeled roof, the stars, dimmed by lights and substantially the same, revolved as always to the rhythm of the restaurant. Only she seemed capable of metamorphosis.

They made a place for her at the circular table. She shone there in her auburn dress, lighting them with her shine, feeling how she was to them. Their faces were her mirrors, would always be.

She tossed a hundred chips into the basket and spoke her color. The uniformed spinner plunged the lever home and the twenty silver balls exploded from their pan to rocket about the curved walls of the table, spurl, and tumble away, spent.

"*Rien*," said the spinner. He glanced about. "*Encore?*"

Around her, hands threw batches of colored chips into the basket. Magdala threw another hundred white.

The lever plummeted, the twenty balls raced. This time three struck the magnets.

"*Rose. Jaune. Et Blanc.*"

Magdala had won. A little applause from the table, the gambler's vicious and taunting tribute to beginner's luck.

"*Encore?*"

"*Changer*," Magdala said. She was now entitled to choose up to a hundred chips of an alternate color from the basket. She showed and dropped back a batch of red.

The lever clanged on its spring, the magnets released their catch, the twenty balls leaped like water from a faucet.

"*Rouge et Rouge. Double remporte.*"

A small teasing cheer this time. A man at Magdala's elbow said, "Lady Luck herself."

"Not quite."

It was Claudio's voice, just behind her. Smoothly he added, "Cash your chips, Magda."

"Not yet," she said. Her own voice was as smooth as his. "*Même*," she called to the spinner.

The lever clanged.

Watching the whirling silver balls, she could visualize the pallor of the man behind her, the raging pallor, the eyes cold as glycerine. Both her arms were jewelessly bare. Five magnets transfixed five spinning balls. The gambler at Magdala's elbow exclaimed. They had both won.

"Your luck rubs off." He brushed her naked shoulder with his finger and licked the finger.

"*Rouge et Vert. Remporte et remporte. Encore?*"

"*Changer*," said Magdala and reached toward the basket.

"*Pas encore*," said Claudio. With finesse he pinioned her wrist, making it look casual, friendly; hurting her. "I said, cash your chips."

"Oh, my God, don't take my luck away," remonstrated the man who had won on the green.

With her free hand, Magdala showed and dropped a hundred batch of yellow in the basket.

"*Même*," said the man beside her. "Like the lady."

"Where is the bracelet?" Claudio said in Magdala's ear.

The lever clanged.

Claudio, still in possession of her wrist, craned forward across the table, scrutinizing the spin.

There was an extended and bitterly satisfied groan all about the table. The balls subsided.

"*Rien*," said the spinner.

"So much for luck," said the man who had won on the green.

"*Encore?*" inquired the spinner.

Magdala set her hand on her scoop to lift a third batch of white chips, but Claudio said loudly: "*Pas encore*. My sister is playing against my account. I cancel. She's already lost me two hundred astrads."

The table murmured.

Claudio shifted his grip to her waist, and marched her away from the spin table. He returned the eight hundred chips to the kiosk, and guided Magdala graciously onto a descending stair.

"Where's the bracelet?"

"Which bracelet?"

He was not pale after all, but his face was a carving, immutable and threatening.

"This is the third phase, is it? Elation followed by

withdrawal followed by idiocy. Where did you learn to play spin?"

"I read about it in books. I've seen it on Tri-V. I could never play before," she said blankly.

"I quite see that." Alone with her on the escalator, he hugged her near, bending to her ear like a lover. "The bracelet."

"You want the recording tape in the clasp, not the bracelet," she said.

He stiffened slightly.

"You're becoming pedantic, Magda. Yes, the tape. Where?"

She felt him start to tremble, whether in his rage or in consternation she was unsure. She was afraid, but with the new fear, different from the old. They traveled down the escalator, jammed together and chained there by his trembling iron hand on her waist.

"At the bottom, we get off. We take the elevator, we go to the suite, and you fetch the bracelet."

"Perhaps it isn't in the suite."

They were ten flowing steps from the ground.

"Magda," he whispered, "it would be so simple for me to kill you. Those leads and wires. . . . You're so very vulnerable, don't risk yourself with me."

Their feet leveled with the ground. They moved, still linked, toward the elevator.

"It must be very important. What Paul Hovak said to me. He called me Christa."

The polished steel door gaped. They were in the elevator and the elevator shot upwards.

"Why," she said, "did he think I was someone called Christa? Do I resemble someone called Christa?" She half turned in the vise of his arm. "You believed, because I was ugly and deformed and sickening to look at, you believed I was a moron."

The elevator deposited them. They went along the corridor. Claudio used the tag to open the door to the suite. They were inside, and the golden lights flooded beautifully into their night-time auspices.

"A moron," she said. "If you only knew," she said, "how much I hate you. All of them. But most of all, you, Claudio."

He swung her around. Her hair cast itself in a shimmering blue-black veil across her face. Her heart throbbed. The thing within her was more vital than her drunkenness had been, and more assured.

His hands were clamped on her skin. Hovak had held her like this. This was, however, different.

"The last time," Claudio said. "Where?"

"The last time," Magdala said. "*Find* it."

He shivered. (Irlin had shivered, not the same.) There was a dark flickering in Claudio's eyes. He had been too confident in his mastery over her. Rebellion had him at a loss.

She was not interested in why he needed the recording tape this desperately. Only in thwarting him.

"I would say," she said gently, "you can't damage me very much as I am. As for killing me—well, you might never get the bracelet then."

"What do you want?" he said.

"I want to see you as you are right now—panic-stricken."

He thrust her away and began to rip the room apart. He whirled the cushions from the chairs, deflated the pneumatics of the chairs themselves, crashed wide all that would open and slung it from him. He passed into her bedroom and tore the dresses from their plastase and their racks. He tipped the carton of perfume sachets on the floor. He dashed the covers from her bed. He rent their seams, and thermo quilting spilled like snow.

His search had already grown systematic, thorough

and sadistic. He vandalized whatever had become hers, all he had given her.

When this was done, he straightened and said to her, his voice fragmentary as the items he had shredded, "Can it be you were sufficiently stupid to hide it in my room?"

"Oh, Claudio," she said, "haven't you considered the disposal mechanism of the lavatories?"

With startled objectivity, she beheld again his brand upon her; Tri-V dialogue had given place to Claudio dialogue. Even the tone was his. Her inventor.

He trod almost delicately through the wreckage of her clothes. In one sinuous, irresistible movement he lifted her off her feet.

She found herself in contact with him once more, plastered to him through both their succession of garments. He carried her to the window, maneuvered her. The window slid upwards even as Claudio slid her outward. The air gushed up like water over her face, her neck, her shoulders, her arms. She was hanging hooked backwards from her bent knees, the rest of her fallen suddenly into nothing but atmosphere. Below, the sea laved the shore, steel on steel and sixty meters down. She could glimpse the piers like gleaming threads stretched out to some invisible bobbin. She herself was anchored merely by Claudio's grasp on her calves.

"Recollect," he said. "An efficient pain cipher can cause your death. I swear I will let you go unless you tell me where the recording tape is. No, I don't accept that you destroyed it. You're enjoying this too much not to be in possession of the ace card."

In the arms which kept her from the abyss, she felt also the tremor of his rage or distress. And, at the same moment, a recalcitrant terrible strength, which would never slough her. Even as he pushed her from the brink, he clung to her.

"Let me up, Claudio," she said, "and I'll tell you."

"No," he said, "oh, no."

She relaxed, gave her weight over to him. It was an abandonment of extraordinary proportions.

"Then, let me go."

She hung there in the silence. If I fall, she thought, it will be for an instant, like flying.

When he drew her slowly and awesomely back, over the ledge of the window, to crumple inside the room, she discovered her eyes had learned to make tears.

He was not breathing. He kneeled in front of her, staring at her.

"The bracelet," she said quietly, "is pinned inside the fringe of the dress I'm wearing."

He started to breathe again, rapidly, as if he could pull chunks of solid oxygen into his lungs.

Magdala parted the undetectable surfaces of the pressure-zip, crossed her hands inside the fringe, and sprung the pins. She offered the bracelet to him.

The sapphires dripped into his hand, and now he stared at these. When he lifted his head, his face had divested itself of everything, or very nearly. Only his youth, his handsomeness, remained in his face, like things stranded in the wake of the storm, things no longer relevant, or alive.

"Magdala," he said, stumbling sluggishly over the name, as if trying to remember it.

The window was automatically and leisurely sealing itself against the cold night, transparent sections striving toward each other in an imperative slow motion.

In the same slow motion, Claudio leaned toward her. His fingers made their contact with her pensively, almost idly, tracing her throat into her jaw, gilding her skin with awakened nerves. As if he explored some unguessed object in a void, dependent on tangible evidence alone, he sent his hands over the surfaces of her skin, her dress, her hair. In the total quiet, their breathing seemed to emanate from a single pair of lungs, prolonged intent gaspings, quite in unison. And, between each gasp, she heard the distant sea.

The window fused. His hands tightened, dragged her. She responded, swimming to him, pulled through deep water; falling into the abyss despite rescue. They met; it was like sanctuary, now, to reach him.

His hands molded her into his body, she could hardly bear the exquisite sensations that attended their passing and re-passing. She shut her eyes to entomb herself in blackness with her pleasure. Filling her mouth with his, he banished the last finite portion of reality. She became a mindless, craving, oceanic beast, deaf and sightless, aware merely through every iota and micro-atom of its flesh. Even her bones seemed to echo his touch. A cave inside her loins opened, opened to the pit of her skull.

They had subsided under the window, twisted among the shattered materials of his search. Something ground in her side—the sapphires.

He had moved her own hand discriminately to discover him. The pulsing tower of his sex beneath her hand increased. Its action fascinated and alarmed her. But he slid her hand from him like a glove. She fell back, clinging to him, as he sheathed himself within her. Invaded, instinctively she struggled, and a golden note resonated through her, a vast shockwave, spreading to the extremities of her limbs and hair.

She opened her eyes then, seeking the cause of the effect.

They rose and sank together in an identical sea. Their faces too were probably identical. It disturbed her to see him. Again she closed her eyes, but with the memory of his face imprinted on her lids, the huge tide began to flood her in a succession of mounting, tumultuous breakers.

"Inside its glazium coffin, the vile deformity has just experienced the sexual crisis your present framework conveyed to it. Neural circuits have engaged, and your brain has relayed that crisis in return to the pseudo-system of your present simulate body. Orgasm by proxy. Odd," Claudio commented softly. "I never once recalled it was *that* I was making love to. But you mustn't overlook the fact, Christa-Magdala, that you are, to coin a phrase, neither here nor there. Don't worry. I won't let you forget. The devil in the box has climaxed and the wires are singing."

She had not wanted him to speak. Exposed, the biting edge of his words scalded her, as plainly it was meant to. The aberration had come and gone. He controlled her again, that was all. Despite the preface, he had claimed from her the most abject obedience.

Besides, in the aftermath, dulled and extinguished, she had reasoned.

"In any case," she said now, "Christa, whoever Christa is, was who you wanted and what you had. I must be very like Christa."

He stood up, disheveled, drained, and bored. The sapphires swung from his fingers.

"Like?" he said mildly. "It's more than that. You're her induced genetic reprint. Deliberately, and literally, her double."

Four

Crossing the Line

I

*I*T'S SEVENDAY OF *the first Dek of the second month of the third quarter,* said the calendar-dial. *Today is Federation day on Earth Conclave Planets Cassandra, Cane, and Pharo. It's the Independence Carnival on Out-Conclave Planet Peace. And on Earth, it's Easter sevenday.*

On Indigo, those who practiced Modernist Christianity would be in their white rectangular churches. The religion of the State Children's Home had been M.C. and one sevenday of every Dek the children had been ushered into the church. Recorded music would play and golden light swell through a false window. The Gregorian letter T, such was the M.C. device, had been photo-processed into the walls and floors. While they sang, the other children had inflicted surreptitious hurts on Magdala, and she had never been able to concentrate. Christ took no notice, which was not surprising, for he too, apparently, was a good-looking man.

Claudio was not in the suite, and she wondered if he were in some church in the hills, praying before the letter T. She knew really nothing about Claudio, but certain aspects of him she might predict, and religious fervor did not suggest itself as one of them.

She did not like to think of him. She could think of him only in two ways—his face above her as their bodies worked beneath the window; the words which followed.

Magdala imagined he had by now listened to the micro-tape in the bracelet and gleaned the expected information. She did not want to reason any further as to what he might wish or what his plans might be. (Perhaps he had made a mistake and some vital clue had not been persuaded from Paul Hovak. Claudio had been very anxious to avoid a personal meeting with Hovak. So anxious, he had trusted to Magdala's presumed ignorance and slavishness. But in the end, that had paid off, had it not?)

She had slept last night, seven hours, an unusually long slumber for her current needs. Which gave rise to the oppressive idea Claudio had tampered again with her body in the capsule, feeding in narcotics as he had fed in spirits. But even this line of questioning she closed off from herself.

Not prone to sleep or hunger, she lay on her pneumatic bed among the torn thermo covers, while all about, the hotel vaguely hummed with the activity of its human and mechanical life.

In the afternoon, she watched a Tri-V drama. One man had murdered another for his wealth, but the murderer's new finances availed him nothing, as he was relentlessly tracked down by an intelligent officer of the detection squad, an archetype who earned only six hundred astrads a month. The undercurrent panacea of the drama was obvious—the erosion of the unfairly favored by the working class was a balm to cash-jealousy.

Claudio entered the suite as the rich murderer, his ambitions ruined, shot himself with an ivory-inlaid delectro. Claudio blacked the screen.

"The rich men must die," he remarked. "The first murdered by one of his confreres, the second hounded to self-destruction by a man of the people. Sometimes the beautiful are required to die, too. You would have liked that best, wouldn't you, Magda?"

He came and sat by her, and as she nervously lifted herself, ran his hands across her body. Her reaction was immediate, neither could she hide it from him. She felt his indifference even as her blood—which was not blood—burned up within her.

"And now," he said quietly, "I can make you do whatever I say. Can't I?"

Her heart, complement to its physical counterpart, was violently beating, and he cupped her breast, only to measure the gallop of the heart, interested. He was not seeing her as Christa now, but as something he had constructed. All this she felt, as she panted like an animal which had been hunted, and lay against him, unable to pull away.

"Can't I?" he repeated. "Very well. You needn't answer. You *are* answering, whether you speak or not."

Presently, he left her, and walked to the window. She balanced her equilibrium precariously, and he gave her, mockingly, the space.

When he resumed talking, it was in the same clinical voice he had used for the recorded lesson at the silver house. Thus enabling her to realize that there was another lesson.

"I suppose, from the beginning, you may have had some notion that my experiment with you was not altruistic, not because I liked you or meant to bring you happiness. And now, having ploughed through all manner of troubles, you may dream I am about to expose the truth to you unequivocally. Make you a mistress of all these dark secret things that seem to be gathering on your life like flies on the jam. But I'm not, Magda. It's a facet of my scheme, your incomprehension. It's already proved an infallible bait with Hovak. What did I want from Hovak? Shall I tell you? Perhaps you can guess. No? Firstly, evidence of his continued collusion with the woman you appeared to him to be, and his preparedness to come running at her call. And what else, I wonder?"

He seemed to be prompting her. Magdala said wearily: "Something he said that the tape recorded."

"Nearly, but not quite."

He had stopped prompting. He would not enlighten her. She did not care. Suddenly he said:

"The most entrancing thing of all was his disgust at confronting the drunken mad lady he supposed was Christophine. By the way, that's her name: Christophine. Not Christa. Christa is the pet abbreviation her colleagues and lovers attempt to reduce her to. Her I.D. reads Christophine del Jan. Try it on for size. You may have to grow into it."

"Whatever you want me to do next," she said, "I might refuse."

"No, you won't." He swung back and smiled at her. "You won't."

She looked beyond him, at the window, but he said, "Firstly, the capsule. I can block your access to it any time I wish. Through its maintenance systems, I can reduce you to a mindless stupor with alcohol or dope. I can also kill you. That's one sound motive for you doing everything I ask. But then, there's the other motive, is there not?"

At which, he came straight to her, and took hold of her, spreading her flesh against his. She tried to push him away, but she had no strength to do it. The textures of him, the scent of him, his mouth and hands and body elicited a scale of terrifyingly unavoidable responses, as if she were some pre-programmed machine set going at the pressure of a key.

Within seconds, she was already flying, blind and helpless, on the wild and downhill race of sex, to be mortally wounded in a collision of light at its finish.

When he let her go, she dropped back and lay immobile and nauseated.

"That's why you'll do what I ask," he said. "And now I'll tell you the very small amount you need to know, and the even smaller amount you'll need to understand."

He told her in a couple of sentences, then slipped the two silver music discs into her ears. She lay there and listened, as they soaped the inside of her mechanical skull with an M.C. religious harmonic for Easter sevenday.

II

NORTH POINT STRETCHED three kilometers into the ocean. A concrete causeway, fenced with concave steel stanchions against the breakers, ran out to a block-built quay. Along the receding shores east and west, the faintly fluorescent pylons marched, emitting their nocturnal pulses of infra-red visible only to the robot guidance of sea traffic.

Elsewhere, beyond the dimmed headlamp of the car, the night was black: black sea, black sky with a seasonal overcast painting out the stars.

There had been five or six M.C. Easter bonfires on the beaches as Claudio drove across the last six hundred and eighty kilometers of Sapphire Flats. But, on the open country rising from the Flats and empty of resort hotels, only the beacon of a single hydraulic powerhouse had leavened the blackness.

The untreated steel stanchions of the causeway had rusted. The quay appeared derelict and seldom used. Yet it was the embarkation point for the place known as Marine Bleu. Claudio had told her what Marine Bleu was, both literally and allegorically. "An E.C. government-sponsored station dedicated to oceanic research. Within this unit, a second unspecified unit. Top secret. Christophine's. But in fact, I perceive Marine Bleu is Circe's island. Where the blue-haired enchantress turns men into beasts."

The car hummed melodiously, poised on the causeway.

"Now we wait, briefly," said Claudio, "until the jet arrives. Meanwhile, it's time for your catechism."

"I remember," she said, through the dark inside the car.

"Maybe you do. Repeat it all the same. Who are you?"

"Christophine del Jan."

"When the jet comes, what do you do?"

"The passenger door and storage bay will open when the autocular mechanism recognizes me. I switch the car to robot-drive and leave the bay to guide it inside. The jet is entirely automatic."

"And isn't that lovely? What about when you reach the island?"

"Any checkposts will respond to my voice and print. The car is pre-programmed to drive me."

"To drive you to the witch's house."

He had requested the aqua-jet from the island by stelex, using Christophine's name. There had also been a code, which Claudio produced and used off-handedly. Demonstrably, Claudio knew Marine Bleu well, its geography, its requirements, its governmental mystique, yet he meant to travel under cover of his fake Christophine, himself in hiding, shut into the back seat-storage compartment of his car. He intended to penetrate the island unseen and unrecorded, like a devil in the dark.

Through the sea-smoothed stillness, the roar of the aqua-jet broke suddenly, prefacing form or lights.

"Only remember, your capsule is locked away and I retain the key. Tomorrow you'll need to service the life-support systems. You've been told what will happen if you're prevented. I stress this, just in case you become skittish. Now, you're on your own."

He depressed the button on the dashboard which raised the back seat of the car, and stepped, with an actor's coordinated economy, into the storage compartment with its interior illumination and washed-air. She recalled how she had floundered into that same compartment on the way north from this city, how she had lain there, sensually possessed, even in her hideousness, by the magic of Claudio's power over her, her power over Claudio. She closed the seat on him now, as he had closed it on her.

She sat in the gloom behind the headlamp. Inside five minutes more, the lights of the aqua-jet burned up from the sea.

When it came in over the ramp of the jetty, with a gush of reducing speed, she switched the car to robot-drive, buttoned up the side, and got out.

The great jet was black as the night, but with luminous red I.D. panels on both sides. The letters ECSORNI glowed above.

The aqua motors sank abruptly in decibels, and the rear and fore sections of the jet opened together. Uncannily, the empty transport yawned there, waiting for her.

She leaned through and activated the starter of the car, shutting the side as she did so. With delicacy, the car drove itself down the ramp and into the rear section of the jet.

Magdala walked to the jet, climbed through and settled herself in the passenger seat behind the automatic instrument board. The side of the jet dropped down and sealed with a velvet thud. The ozone of the washed-air percolated the cabin, the motors thrust, and the jet rose on its gas cushion.

Moments after, it plunged into the sea, vents sucking up water, evacuating water in a strong white wake. The speedometer danced through fifty, one hundred, two hundred, kph.

There were red letters to the left of the panel, the same letters as on the external I.D.: ECSORNI. She knew what they stood for: Earth Conclave Station, Oceanic Research, Northern Indigo.

She thought of Claudio, shut in the storage compartment, her companion; yet not her companion. Vaguely, she liked the idea of Claudio impotently trapped in this way, at the mercy of her obedience.

But, alone in the dark as the jet carved the night into a deeper darkness, and the polarized screen grew flecked with black liquid drops, she began to think only of Claudio, as if his soul ate hers, as if she had no life at all, save through him.

Northward and farther north the aqua-jet darted, a flung spear of water and noise through the night.

Northward, Fall had already reached Indigo. Fall when all the blue leaves fell, and the sky deepened, and the pre-winter storms came blowing in like the blue-black whales that had once billowed through the blue seas, before Earth Conclave had dispatched them to five hundred zoos and five thousand research faculties. There were no longer whales on earth, few animal species of any sort. Mother Gaea. Her sons left her for other worlds: they sent her presents and never went home.

In the second hour of the journey, a storm spoke on the horizon ahead, out across the dance floor of the sea.

The jet, catching up to the storm, weatherproofed and motored with a peak of pollution-timid clean technology, clove through the waves and the thick wind like a blade through black butter.

The storm remedied her dreary abnegation somewhat, as if its spark touched off some circuit within herself. But the token thought of her rebellion at this time was merely a hope that Claudio, the scintillant magician, suffered ennui, unentertained in the seat-storage of the car.

The island emerged out of the sea at three in the morning. Its pivot was a tall conical cliff, muffled in a static cloud of forest. For six or seven kilometers from the base of the cliff to the water, there extended a uniformly flat plain, featureless but for the blocks and boxes of buildings, and a chain of stalking infra-red pylons.

As the jet soared closer, Magdala discerned that the flat plain was a reinforced concrete apron, a man-made adjunct to the island—which was no more than the conical cliff.

A kilometer from land, the jet swept into a left hand maneuver, turning from the docking basin of the station, and ploughing north westward around the saucerene curve of the concrete foreshore. In less than a minute, the uncompromising blocks were out of sight. The spindle of the forested cliff towered above the apron, which itself presently surrendered to a turmoil of sea. Large rocks, outposts of the cliff, clawed from the water, breakers salivating ferociously between them. The jet shot through a narrow channel, white-winged with surf, and ran up a treated metal ramp.

The motors subsided to an intermediary rumble. But, in the partial silence, the ocean asserted itself, waves hurled loudly against rock, slithering back with smashed spines, then, healed by immersion, hurled forward again.

Ahead and above, a metal road plunged off from the ramp and straight up the cliff, burying itself in the trees.

Magdala heard the jet's storage bay open and Claudio's car drive out. It moved along the flank of the jet and pulled up on the road, and the door section of the jet lifted.

The sea screamed. The night smelled dank and oddly

menacing with salt, as if the ghost of a great ocean beast moved through it, breathing.

Magdala slid down from the cabin and walked toward the car. Once she was off the ramp, it began to sink, carrying the aqua-jet into some concrete shed underground. This vanishing trick struck her curiously, with intimations of impermanence. Where the car had halted, a cement pillar had been set beside the road. A light stammered in the pillar, and, as she came nearer an ab-human voice demanded dulcetly: *Print and voice check, please.* She put her hand on the print plate. *Voice, please,* said the pillar. *Voice, please.* A fleeting impulse to offer her own—wrong—name. Stifled. "Christophine," she said, "del Jan." The blue light faded. *Check,* the pillar said. "*Fool,*" she thought. "*Fool.*"

At the base of the cliff, just before the trees smothered the road, huge leprous wounds gaped in the rock, each an unspeakable invitation into blackness.

Despite the road, the ramp, the checkpost, there was nothing civilized about the back door into Marine Bleu. It was a country of caves, decay, and supernatural anger.

She got into the car, and the howling of the sea was muffled. The car started up the fluorescent road, mounting the dark cone into the roll of the trees.

Claudio, lying in the compartment, at the mercy of her obedience, and of the button that would release him, which was on the dash. She could savor that. If she wanted, she could talk to him and he would have to hear.

She did not talk.

The forest was quiet, too. Until a strong wind manifested itself, higher on the cliff. A strong fall wind, the harbinger of the storm the jet had out-paced on the ocean. The fringes of the storm might brush the island, and she wondered how much weather control operated here, and what restrictions applied to it.

Shortly, it occurred to her that the trees were not mit-
igating the wind, nor did their branches move or their
foliage—the ephemeral leaves of fall—shake loose. Soon
after, she glimpsed a compact steel unit at the roadside
with the inscription: Hol. Panel Housing 9: Active. Holostets, instigated by electronics. The forerunner of
Claudio's model? But to this, Claudio's model was child
to giant. The visual and tactile mirage of a collective
forest, kilometers deep, projected in order to clothe the
barren slopes of the cliff. Ornament, or disguise?

Precisely then, the wing-tip of the storm flickered
over the island.

There was a bellow of thunder, chalked by lightning.

Magdala cried out.

One moment the world was matte, then, as the white
crack of lightning hit the nonexistent tops of the trees,
they exploded into fires.

The holostetic forest was acting as one vast lightning
absorber, attracting, defusing, and storing the electricity
of the storm. The process had an outlandish side effect
of brilliant color. Fountains of viridian and turquoise
and rose-red light poured down the motionless sinews
of the trees; magenta convolutions became silent purple
snows; blue coronas broke and fell in lime-green rain.

Unaware, the car shot through it, while, spread on the
dash, Magdala's hands gained transparent gauntlets of
violet and crimson; while, like infernal sweets, carna-
tion and quince candied and dissolved on the polarized
windscreen. Between the tree shapes on her left, a concrete bungalow appeared, reflectively neoned jade,
pink, royal blue. And presently, three more bungalows,
winking topaz, peacock's eye, vermilion, mazerine.

The whole interior of the car was dyed and re-dyed a
hundred variables of color. Then, the frenetic patterns
distilled, faltered. There had been no further lightning.
The glowing fires of Hell were seeping back into the

cliff. Almost as suddenly as it had commenced, the display ended. Dyes dying out on every side. Retinas jangled, still stippled with after-images, Magdala beheld a fourth bungalow, showing its prosaic dun format in the headlamp.

The storm, sucked dry of its inshore violence by the hungry holostetic shield, crumpled away with dim boomings into the slavering sea. The wind failed.

The fourth bungalow slid behind like the others, as night collapsed on the forest.

"You missed something then, Claudio," Magdala said aloud. "But probably you've seen it all before."

The sparks of the storm had again ignited her, precipitated her. But her fear, reborn, smote on the pliable insecurity within her. She had come through rainbow flames that did not burn, among trees that were not trees, and she at their heart, not who she seemed either, nor *what* she seemed.

Nothing is to be relied on, Claudio had said to her, at the beginning. It had turned out to be the litany of their enterprise.

Five minutes later, out of the black, a fifth bungalow, columen-built. The pre-programmed car slowed, swam toward the bungalow. Christophine's bungalow.

It was quite unlike the previous structures, and not only because the electric suffusion of color was gone. The earlier buildings had had the prefabricated boxlike style of the blocks in the Research Station compounds.

The columen bungalow was upheld on its steel columns at a height of four and a half meters, the central support being a drum-shaped garage faced with copper cladding. The living area sat on its stilts, an octagon up in the air, with the dome of a solarium roof above. The car headlamp shone wetly black on the one-way glazium, which might or might not shine an equally opaque gold if somebody were home.

The car stopped.

Magdala sat in the car, her attention fixed on Christophine's bungalow.

Entry to the bungalow could be procured via the garage. Entry to the garage through an activating key in the car of Christophine del Jan. The magician, however, could no doubt effect entry by other means.

The time had come, therefore, to button up the back seat and allow the magician to return into the world.

It was like having a virus trapped in a sealed jar. A beautiful, aesthetic, seductive virus. A plague. A malediction. Satan. A wonderful irrationality, devoid of concession, bathed her nerves. "Can you still hear me, Claudio?" she said. "I am debating with myself whether to let you out. Or not. Of course, I suppose I could leave you there indefinitely. That would be rather awkward for you, would it not? Would rather spoil your plans."

She shut her eyes and imagined Claudio's face eclipsed by panic as she had seen it the night before. And then she became aware that he never would have trusted her in this. She was aware even before she heard the slight hiss of contained atmosphere escaping from the back seat as it lifted. He had his own device for freeing himself when the hour of freedom arrived. How had she ever dreamed it could be otherwise? The split seconds of autonomy, as ever, evaporated.

She did not look about.

For his part, he did not speak to her, but reached by her to the panel to raise the rear side section of the car.

She watched him walk between the steel columns, under the bungalow, to the garage. She could picture the silver rectangle with which he had effortlessly got into her apartment at the Accomat. On this occasion, she was not shown what he used, but the curving slide-door of the garage retreated, leaving the way open.

He came back to the car, into the front beside her, and drove forward into the garage.

"There's also a print-lock which will think it recognizes your thumb, and let you in," he said, conversationally.

Just as conversationally, she inquired: "Will you leave the car here?"

"No."

She was surprised he had bothered to answer.

"Where, then?"

He had stopped the car, and the garage door was closing. A white light bloomed in the garage. Claudio half-turned, half-looked at her. His eyes seemed capable of hypnotism.

"No more questions," he said. "See the elevator over there? It connects the garage with the bungalow. We'll take the elevator and go up. I'll make love to you on her bed."

Magdala's heart jumped in its pseudo, totally mortal fashion, blurring her sight, making her catch her breath. Not even touching him, she already writhed at his touch, the downhill race already begun inside her lungs, her loins, her skull.

"My reward for compliance?" she asked.

"Well, you'll feel rewarded. Won't you?"

She said: "Christophine's simulate on Christophine's bed. Why did you bring me here?"

"Still questioning? Disobedience cancels the reward," he said coldly.

But she saw the pulse in his throat, his temple. Not beating as fast as hers, yet beating, beating. She leaned forward. Her hair swung to enclose both their faces. She brushed his lips with hers and said to him: "But I'm Christophine, darling." She moved her hand down his body. She did it cunningly. She had learned method from him. "You're already much too excited at the idea of Christophine's bed. Aren't you, darling?"

Ten minutes later, the sequence begun in the car was completed on a strange swaying couch, slung hammock-wise from four flexium suspensors.

As the bed swung like a huge pendulum, and she flung herself through all the glistening cascades of physical emotion, Magdala wondered how many times he had made love to Christophine. A sensation of being partially out of her body came over her, so that her climax was a separate thing, observed almost dispassionately. She heard her own voice rising thin and wild, like the voice of someone in another room. She sounded as though she were being hurt. Which obscurely puzzled her.

She regained herself in stages, and lay in the dim room, where just one shadowy light had spontaneously lit itself, with her enemy beside her. Already the music discs were in his ears, churning out their hackneyed and saccharine formulae.

"What now?" she said.

He could not have heard her, though he registered that she had spoken.

"Shut up," he murmured. "Shut up."

Plangently, Christophine's bed swung beneath them.

III

THE OCTAGONAL BUNGALOW was about fifteen meters in diameter, mostly open-plan in design. A boxed-in bathroom unit ran along the large southeast section of the octagon, and a boxed-in eating area and kitchen occupied the western section, equipped with facilities for creative cooking Magdala had never seen before, save in Tri-V movies.

The suspended bed hung in the southern portion of the octagon. You could lower it to the highly glossed cushion floor, or elevate it a full two meters.

The bronze lift shaft ran straight through the room at its center, giving access to the garage below, or the solarium above on the roof. The solarium was filled with tawny summer plants and the dark blue plants of the Blue season. It could be flooded by the sunlight of solar batteries and it could be made to rain at the loosening of a valve. There were panes of colored glass in the dome.

The colors of the bungalow were predominantly coffee, shades ranging from a roasted milkless black to café crème. On this coffee scheme, blue sugars had been scattered, azure bolsters embroidered with golden birds,

and cyanide vases. A glazium chimney near the east
wall would burn decorative deflaminate fires—blue for
summer refreshment, red for winter cheer. Nothing in
the bungalow was purely functional.

All the window-walls looked out upon the forest, but
could be rendered opaque, as in Claudio's silver house.
On investigation, Magdala had found only the northern
wall set as a window. Before this window stood a piece
of gigantic mahogany furniture, mirrored panther-black
in the burnished cushionings beneath: a contrachorda.
Magdala opened the button panel in its side and thumbed
down the release button. The fore-lid pleated back to
expose a translucent ivory keyboard. The upper lid rose,
lifting the strings, in their trough of hammers, from the
instrument's interior. When the strings were stretched,
she pressed the tuning button and observed their pliant
surfaces slacken and tauten, like wings exercising. And
then, she could do no more than paddle her fingers up
and down the keyboard, seeing the silver hammers hit
the golden strings, listening to the clear pitched notes,
detonated like crystal beads into the room. She could not
play, had never been tutored. This hybrid of the harps
and pianos and celestinas of Earth remained mute, or at
least incoherent, under her hands.

Throughout all this, Claudio lay on the bed, awake,
deaf, and reticent.

She sat on the stool before the contrachorda, in the
minimally lit bungalow, whose lights could be switched
on and off at will. She compared, irresistibly and precisely, how the woman Christophine lived, and how
Magdala Cled had lived. An Accomat apartment, four
by three meters, with a bathroom cubicle half that size,
and a food-dial on the wall the only way of fixing food.

And a fur cat for company in a bed that unfolded
from the wall.

She slept and woke and dawn was seeping through the holostet forest.

Claudio sat, regarding her. His face was sharp. The music discs were not in his ears. Like Christ, he had come back out of the wilderness to teach her her path. But not like Christ. Not at all.

"Do you hate her yet?" This was the first thing he said to her. "I mean, do you hate Christophine del Jan? All these items in her possession which you never had. You hate *me* for my possessions, don't you?" His voice was lazy. Again and again it seemed he read her thoughts. Could he? His creature ... "Hate her, Magda. She has the ultimate item which you should covet. The duplicate of your flesh. Speaking of flesh, you'd better go down to the garage and clean out your cage."

She stared at him.

"Well, go on. You know how the chassis-storage works. It's the eighth day of the cycle. The instructions are on the side of the capsule."

She got up stiffly and walked to the elevator.

When she returned twenty minutes later, her eyes were wet and her hands shook. He registered her demeanor with intrigued irony.

"Salt in the wound, was it?"

Despite that most intransigent evidence before her eyes that her present body was not her own and that her insides were therefore stable, she had been retching. Retching as she energized the simple systems in the capsule, to cleanse and sustain. She had gazed at herself a mere three nights before, at Sugar Beach, gazed with a sort of morbid derision. The intimacy of service to the form in the capsule, however, obviated her aloofness. She was shocked at her own reaction.

"Now you can really hate Christophine," he said. "Her skin's her own. How about it?"

She found she hated Christophine. A terrified primordial hate. To evade the issue, she said:

"You don't know when she'll be here. Or do you?"

"I don't. Exhilarated by the prospect?"

"But you knew she wouldn't be here now."

"I knew that. Shall I let you in on the secret? I shall. Christophine is interested in my whereabouts. So I sent her a stelex. *Claudio*, it unequivocally said, *is in Saint Azoro*. No doubt Christophine is in Saint Azoro this minute, hunting me up and down the boulevards, snarling like a tiger. *Don't* ask me why."

"And when she doesn't find you, she'll come back to the island."

"Let's not burden ourselves with hypotheses."

"Claudio—" she said.

"Yes?" Amenable, amiable, he beamed at her, and all initiative withered.

"What am I supposed to do here," Magdala whispered, "now I am here?"

"Have fun. Play with Christophine's objets d'art. Amuse yourself."

"But," she faltered, "what will you do?"

"I? Oh, I'll be about. Going to and fro, walking up and down. Take no notice of me. All I request is that you don't forget I shall have taken the car and secreted it somewhere, and in the car is your worse half under lock and key. Insurance."

She sat down beside the contrachorda. He had shut the two lids. She leaned her cheek on its planed and silken wood.

Claudio rose and approached her through the northern spotlight of the dawn window.

"Hate," he said. "Worlds have been conquered on the strength of that. Hate me, Magdala, but hate her more." He put his hand gently on her head. Gently he said to her, "Share it with me, Magdala. My hate for Christophine."

"Why?" she said.

"I informed you, you must not ask why, or what. You are my marionette. Dance for me, and keep your mouth shut. Or I won't be nice to you anymore."

The idea of his being, of all absurdities, *nice*, made her laugh, but the laugh, as if also his slave, was silent.

The light clasp of his hand upon her head was shortly released. He left her, and soon she heard the growl of the car as it drove away into the steel-blue morning.

By nine-thirty the sun was over the lower trees of the forest. She had cleared the glazium of the northeastern and eastern walls of the octagon to let daylight into the bungalow. The holostets of the higher trees fenced the sun but could not impede it. It slashed them wide and spilled through, a round of brilliance, and no shadows barred the polished floor. But she had made an odd discovery: a solitary bona fide tree grew on the bungalow's northern side. Its leaves had long since blued and abandoned it. Its trunk had reverted to the pale tan color of winter, spring, and summer. Its shadow ran along the ground. The rest of the trees, the false trees, were inexorably a dark sullen shade. The solar generator murmured on the solarium roof.

Claudio was gone. He had taken her clothes, all those expensive dresses and separates which he had bought for her. He had taken her clothes in order that she would have to wear Christophine's.

She showered, and shampooed her hair. In the middle of shampooing, she visualized the monster in the coffin, and herself in a robot body. A doll, bent to the basin, suds in its hair. She imagined all of the navy hair depilating in the basin. But it did not. She knew it would not, having shampooed it before. She was a doll which could be bathed, with washable tresses. She was a doll who could walk and talk, and eat and drink and sleep, and have orgasms.

The clothes closet was in the floor near the bed, raised by a key in the panel next to the south window-wall. The closet rose and its door sank. Here hung the garments of Christophine, like a line of flayed skins.

She did not want to wear Christophine's clothes.

She wanted to—

She wanted to rip them. She wanted to rip and tear—

Not only the clothes, the bungalow.

Christophine.

The revelation was flamboyant. She had been stalling, avoiding whatever oblique retaliation Claudio had designated for her. Claudio wanted her to hate Christophine so that she would fulfill some yearning of Claudio's own. But Magdala's hate was indigenous to Magdala. She hated them both and her criteria were personal.

Cautiously, she drew the nearest dress from its plastase. It was a burnt-sienna dress of shepra wool. She carried it into the kitchen area and laid it down. Taking one of the bizarrely antique and very sharp cook's knives, Magdala slit the dress in two segments.

As the blade parted the final threads, a voice floated through the open plan of the bungalow.

Someone is here. Someone is here.

Magdala dropped the pieces of the dress and the knife. She crept from the kitchen area.

An eyelet of light was flashing off and on in the bronze elevator shaft. Above the light, in a little panel, a picture had formed. It showed an unknown man standing between the steel stilts of the bungalow and the black stilts of the forest. He was looking up eagerly, waiting to come in.

Five

Secundo

I

"CHRISTOPHINE," the man said, looking up. "Christophine. Hello?"

There was a chance that if she ignored the man he would leave. The two-way switch beside the vision plate was off; the visitor could not see into the bungalow. Could not see her standing there, naked, petrified, staring at him.

How did he know she was here? Christophine was *not* here.

"Oh, come on, Christa," said the man impatiently, resorting to the abbreviation Claudio had dissected in such detail. "Christa" indicated a colleague. Or a lover. "I do know you're in," said the man, as if he had read her mind. "I saw your lights last night. You're back sooner than I expected. Satiety? Or was it a hunch?"

Below the two-way switch was a button marked *Voice*. Magdala discovered she had pressed it in.

"That *is* you, isn't it, Christa?"

"Yes," she said. And felt dizzy, revolted. Yet again she had fallen, been pushed, or voluntarily leaped from the precipice. Probably pushed. She was certain that

Claudio could have foreseen this, and had perhaps gambled on it, for his own unorthodox reasons.

"Are you coming down, or do I get asked up?"

She did not want him to enter the bungalow. The feeling was instinctive but irrational.

"Give me a minute. I'll come down."

He shrugged.

Perforce then, Magdala donned Christophine's clothes, her lingerie, a white zipless dress, shoes. In a drawer within the closet were perfume sachets, identical to those Claudio had bought her. Magdala avoided them.

Claudio, leaving, had sent the elevator up again. She stepped into it and descended to the garage. The silver car, of course, was gone. The garage door opened as she went toward it.

Outside, the day was palely warm, folded in the blue wrapper of the spurious trees. The man stood smoking in the sunlight. Close to, he was not remarkable, possessor of the usual ordinary, attractive face, but his eyes were rather small, rather dry and flinty. He dropped the self-lighting, self-dousing cigarette on the ground, and nodded to her.

"Was it a hunch?"

"What?" she asked. She did not know his name.

"Whatever brought you back so quickly. It's bad news."

"Is it?"

"Isn't it always? We've got trouble with Emilion."

"Oh," she said, "oh, Emilion." Suddenly she had to suppress a smile. This was farcical. She wondered if Claudio was anywhere about, hiding behind a tree (the smile seduced her again). Maybe he had installed some device, in the bungalow or here in the open, through which he could watch her. He was unwholesomely clever with mechanical gadgets.

"Well, we assumed it would go wrong again, did we not?"

"Yes, I suppose we did," she answered dutifully.

"Do you want to come in and confirm it for yourself, Christa? I'd say you should."

"I don't think," she began. Her mood altered its character abruptly. Running blindfold, she had been bound to lose her footing.

"I've parked the auto by the road," the man said.

"I have a lot of things to attend to here," she said.

"Come on, Christa. Don't cat about. You're in charge of this thing and you damned well should have stayed with it. You want to be a star with the C.T. project, O.K. But it works both ways. When the sweet goes sour, you're not going to land me with holding the can. The others, perhaps. But not Val."

She laughed stupidly. He had gifted her with his name.

Had Claudio prophesied that the man would try to coerce her into going with him? Abruptly, she beheld a bizarre logic in what Claudio meant to happen, through her and through the events which would gravitate toward her. Claudio had said, *"It's a facet of my scheme, your incomprehension."*

It was not just a matter of amusing herself on Marine Bleu. Why should it be? It was a matter of Magdala being mistaken for Christophine as frequently as possible. And of Magdala, in her confused ignorance, presenting a new picture of the hated Christophine—as a mad woman. And how else could it be? She could not help doing it. Claudio's plan could not fail.

She had even laughed, out of context, as a mad lady should.

Peculiarly, though, the man called Val had not taken her laugh as questionable. His dry flinty little eyes had become drier, flintier, more contracted. He licked his lips and said:

"Yes, it's funny now. Maybe not tomorrow."

His attitude, his mannerisms, displayed trepidation and unease. He had told her Christophine was in charge of a project at Marine Bleu. The top secret project Claudio had, uninformatively, digressed upon.

"Don't threaten me," Magdala said to Val. She said it in a friendly way, Claudio's way. It worked. Val shrank in one virtually non-physical yet quite picturesque motion.

"All right, all right. I retract. Shall I kneel?"

"If you would like to."

Val chuckled, demonstrating that this had all been a boyish prank, not a trial of strength between them.

"Same Christa. Always the same."

Rather than laugh this time, she shivered. She thought, inchoately, that Claudio's plan could fail after all. If she could bluff it out. To thwart Claudio. That was important. It always had been, would be. She could hate Christophine, yes. But in her own fashion, because of her own motives. She did not even know what Claudio's motives were.

"What I'm postulating, tentatively and respectfully," said Val, "is that in my capacity as your sub, I'd advise you take a look at Emilion for yourself. That's it."

Magdala ran her eyes along the ranks of the trees to where she could glimpse the auto-cab between. She could say "no." Although obviously Christophine would not say "no."

A buzzing noise came from the direction of the auto.

"Oh God," said Val. He ran off toward the car, and Christophine followed him, without hurry. When she reached the spot, Val was seated inside the open cab, talking into a pin-head mike attachment on the dash. "Yes," he said, "yes." He angled himself to face her. "Worse than I judged," said Val. "I have to get back."

"I'll come with you."

She had reacted blindly to his imperative agitation, to curiosity, to an underlying fear of Claudio and an aversion to continued loneliness at the bungalow. To a surge of frustrated power, wrath, and temper. To the aura of Christophine herself.

She got into the cab and the side closed down.

Too late now to escape.

They were on the metal road, in robot-drive, whirling up the crest of the cliff, under an arch of steel-ribbed natural stone, through the shadowless blaze of the sun-shattered forest. The concrete apron appeared below, a bald and clinical paragraph between the dark upland and the blue lowland of the sea.

They seemed to fall toward the station.

Val did not talk to her, withered by her proximity.

She was strangely disturbed by the calmness of the ocean on this side of the island, reminded of the savage, rock-smashed breakers the jet had reconnoitered the night before. This side, the sea appeared dead.

A quarter kilometer from the station, they passed an auto-check which flashed them through without having them reduce speed. A few moments more, and the cab dashed among the tall and featureless buildings.

She had no time to assess the functional cement prairie of the apron, the blocks, the compounds. Everything flew at her and away.

The auto slowed in the sudden deceleration of robot-drive, throwing up its air barrier within to cushion the occupants, so the cessation was not felt but only seen—a landscape racing by at two hundred kph, abruptly flowing into stasis.

The auto was on a steel pad in a windowless walled precinct. Red panels blazed on the wall, flushed to blue, went out. The pad began to sink.

Overhead, the ground closed.

On its steel platform, the auto descended into a cavern of whitewashed concrete. The hum of many generators swelled through the screens of the auto, which were winding themselves down, and a cold efficient light radiating from Eterna phosphor lamps. There was the inevitable scent of washed-air, phosphix, and the alcohol-chemical smell of a laboratory.

A steel door blocked the end of the cavern. At a guess, the route leading back into the cliff.

The auto side lifted.

A cement pillar stood by the steel door, replica of the pillar at the rock jetty. The same ab-human voice hailed them.

You are at the entrance of Two Unit. Only classified executives will be admitted. Print and voice check, please.

Val went forward quickly, pressing his hand to the pillar, giving his name. Magdala repeated the action. She was beginning to experience the pressure of her situation, a tightening of ghostly rivets and joints in the ozone. But the pillar, predictably, made no demur.

The steel door slid aside.

A corridor of peach plastic, starkly lit by Eternas, opened in front of her, and she grew numb, dumb, eyes unfocused, hands frozen. She did not want to walk into this sanctum, among things she did not understand, people she had never seen, and let them catch her out. And they must catch her out.

She had to fail. She knew nothing—*nothing*.

And this was exactly what Claudio would have wanted.

Together, she and Val moved into the corridor, and along it to a blank wall marked ECSORNI DEUX, which, accepting their images, cracked wide before them.

This area was much as she would have anticipated—the Tri-V drama laboratory. A computer bank the length of one long wall and from floor to ceiling, with a walkway running along the upper case. Computer-linked machinery of process and analysis. Hygienic slabs, a diascope, cabinets of instruments, a book screen, internal televisor, and slotted panels of tapes. In the midst of the area stood five men and two women in indigo blue loose-coats. All of them gazed at her, the expressionless gaze rendered to authority like tax.

"M. del Jan," one of the men said. "Glad to see you back."

She had only to read him to discover her anticipated persona. Remote and implacable, that was Christophine. (Yes, she would have to be that way for Magdala's mistakes to recast her as insane.) Magdala inclined her head to the man who had spoken to her. Val was moving on, but dawdling worriedly in order not to let her drop behind. She joined him, and they passed through a second door.

This room was twice the size of the previous one. There were flexium leads through from the computer bank, and a smaller daughter-bank connected to a desk console. A woman sat at the desk. The rest of the room supported five internal televisors, each monitored by personnel in loose coats seated beneath. Magdala glanced into these televisors, but Val was continuing toward another wall door, permitting her no leisure to absorb visual evidence from the screens, despite the fact that the activity in them was minimal. In one, a man lay, apparently sleeping, on a plastase couch. In another, a woman was propped irregularly in a chair. Someone was coaxing, or seemed to be coaxing, the woman to lift her arm. A grim aura of an archaic lunatic asylum overhung these scenes. Nobody in this room had spoken, shoulders cast-iron as they kept their vigil.

The door gave on to an elevator. It plunged about six meters farther into the sub-surface rock of the cliff. They emerged into a duplicate of the second room above. This room too had computer leads and a daughter-bank, but of the five screens, only one was live. Before the screen, on their feet, restless and conveying impotent emotions, a mixed group shook itself about to greet the arrivals.

"How is he now?" Val barked.

"Bad, M. Valary." The girl who answered turned to Magdala. "M. del Jan, it started early this morning, about six o'clock. I have it logged. Since eight we've been using twenty a.c.s of paramyoten every hour to try to control the behavior pattern, but it hasn't been successful."

Magdala had stopped looking at the girl. She was looking at the screen. In the screen was a rampaging animal that had formerly been a man. From the stretched black oval of the mouth wafted faint cottonwool screamings, muffled by silencers. And as he screamed, the man catapulted himself from one end of his almost featureless chamber to the other.

"Christ," said Valary, "it *is* worse."

"That isn't all," said the girl. "Watch—there, you see?"

The man in the screen had paused beside a wall. Quite systematically, he began to crash his head against it.

"Who's monitoring the subject capsule?" demanded Valary.

"Doramel."

"How are the life signs?"

"Low. Getting lower."

"Christophine," said Valary, looking only at the man in the screen, "do we increase the paramyoten?"

"M. del Jan," said a young man at the edge of the group, "Emilion's subject is already heavily sedated. The feed-drip's been clogged with analgens for three days. The subject can't scrape any nourishment from it anymore."

"Dammit," said Valary, "we have to take the risk. Much more of this, and he'll go into shock. My God, our only logged transfer to date. We really thought we could make it with Emilion. Thirty a.c.s of paramyoten, Christophine?"

Magdala was balancing on a thin line of ice, above a rushing fall of water. She was toppling into the water. She spoke to Valary, unable to resist herself. "What does he mean, the feed-drip's clogged with analgens?"

"Sorry about that, M. del Jan," said the young man, slightly shrinking. "I don't like it, either. But the transfer's become consistently violent. And that's been with a steady five a.c.s of paramyoten in the drip. I'm afraid the motor nerves have gone into spasm. I doubt if we can stop it now, short of actually poisoning him anyway."

"There's no choice," Valary snapped. His dry eyes had grown moist; wet flints. "Jesus—Christophine."

"Do you want to inspect the subject capsule, M. del Jan?" the girl inquired.

Magdala gasped as waters knit over her head. "Why not."

The girl did something to the desk console, and a door gaped. Magdala apprehended she was meant to go through into the cell beyond.

In the cell, a safe had been pulled from the wall. On the horizontal of the safe lay a transparent lozenge. A girl bowed to it, as if in worship.

"Doramel, M. del Jan's coming through."

Doramel straightened. Neat and dark, she offered Magdala a tiny bow.

Magdala walked into the cell, and lowered her eyes till they rested on chill glazium.

The capsule was just like her own, just like the glazium "coffin" Claudio had put her in when she was Ugly. And the arrangement was sufficiently similar so that she could see no disparity. Wires, tubes, coils, a panel of lights (flickering now, not entirely like hers, after all). Yes, and the man in the capsule was different too. He was young, and he was normal. Straight limbs, regular features. On his head was a silver cage.

Magdala put her hand over her face. She was not sure why. The gesture did not ease her. She went on seeing behind her shut lids.

She could not debate. She struggled with a nonsensical, all-pervading horror. The research project special to Two Unit was that identical project Claudio had successfully effected through herself. The transfer of mental consciousness from a human body to a simulate. And, unlike Claudio, Two Unit had failed.

"On paper," said neat dark Doramel, "it works. Doesn't it, M. del Jan? And on the computer it works, too. But we get this. We make the transfer. They stick. We can't get them re-aligned with their original subject bodies, and we can't get them to work their transfer bodies. Emilion was the unit's solitary partial success. He could actually eat and drink and count up to thirty-three. I admit, that always puzzled me, that counting up to thirty-three, no further. But we all admire the labor and skill you've put into this, M. del Jan. I'm sorry."

There was a distant walled-off bellowing.

Somewhere near, Emilion was gouging his steel cranium on the conveniently hard walls.

As they watched, the flickering lights on the capsule panel erupted. Then blacked out.

A series of emergency stimulators took over within the glazium. Oxygen spouted. Air bursts pounded on the heart, blocked the nostrils, forced the lungs to fill and let them sag. Adrenaline canceled the analgens in the feed. But the plaque of lights stayed vacant, and so did Emilion.

Presently a thin whining issued from the life-support maintenance systems as they switched themselves off. There was nothing left to maintain.

Valary wiped his forehead in the outer room.

"Autopsy," he said to the young man. "Code X.6: Emilion K. Diascope and X-ray section. Set up sterilization." He would not glance in Magdala's direction. "All right, Christophine. Do you want to carve the joint, or shall I?"

Bile came into her throat. Even though it could not, it did. But it had a clinical taste, dispassionately clean.

"You do it," Magdala said.

"Very well."

She had been able to notice, the true body in the capsule and the simulate body were perfectly alike, twins. In this instance, there had been no requirement to improve on the frame of this particular subject.

Valary had moved up to her in the cell. Lowering his tone, he said:

"Of course, you reckoned you'd make your name with Emilion. Rotten luck, Christa. Suits you."

Magdala brushed by him, and started to move across the room.

He had sensed her distress, and without guessing its well-spring, fastened on it voraciously. Loudly he called after her, "You know who we need? We need Claudio Loro."

Magdala seemed to meet a barrier in her path. Unable to progress, she turned about.

"What?"

Valary's face flushed, but he had gone too far at last to retreat.

"I shouldn't mention him? My apologies, but he was the king, wasn't he? Too much cash, and too clever. We'd have this in the bag by now, if Loro had stayed with the project."

There was a thick, listening, emphatic stillness in the room.

"Wait a minute," Magdala said. She walked back toward Valary slowly.

But again came one of those non-physical utter collapses.

"Hell, Christophine. I'm out of line. Forget I said it."

"I want," she said, "you to go on telling me about Claudio."

She was slipping further and further from her role, yet preposterously, again her phraseology was wrongly translated as sarcasm and menace. Valary changed tactics startlingly. He held up his hands in mock terror, the sweat of disappointment, fury, and intimidation glistening above his dry moist eyes. Even in her intolerable condition, Magdala spotted the double game—his parody of self-defense which let everyone see Christophine's grip crumbling.

"Val," she said, "I recommend you get on with the work at hand. I'm returning to the bungalow. If you have an inspiration, you can call me."

She turned once more and entered the elevator.

She remembered the progression of the rooms and got through them, and through the polite greetings of their occupants.

She left Two Unit and stood there in the enormous phosfix-smelling cavern, wondering how to reach the surface. When an auto-cab drove toward her and lifted its side to let her in, she complied without any impulse whatsoever. But the cab had remained programmed to her probable locations, the unit and the bungalow. Without any further guidance it drove her on to the metal pad, ascended into the surface compound, and proceeded through the station.

She sat in the cab, dazed, her eyes repelled by concrete vistas. No human figures were visible. She had only a curious perception of blue sky, blue sea; blue mortifying edgings to a bloodless gray concrete mass, incapable of caries.

She cried in the cab, not knowing why. And as the car parted the holostetic forest, she thought of the shut-bed in the Accomat, and Magdala Cled sprawled on it, ugly and misshapen, nursing the toy cat, fear just a shallow water at the bottom of her life.

II

IT WAS NOON, thirteen hours, when, by use of her Christophine thumb print, she walked into the columen bungalow.

She had nowhere else to go.

She had become accustomed to insecurity and craziness. Insecurity and craziness had become familiar and normal. In an existence where nothing offered her safety, no one thing seemed any more dangerous than the rest.

There had been an insistent, half-drawn notion, occurring on the road up the cliff. It had something to do with getting off the island, returning to the mainland—seeking shelter in the city, or some other populated zone. The notion, of course, was absurd. She could not escape, not without her own glazium capsule and its contents.

She had been caught out, again, supposing the sum and total of herself to be this body she seemed to occupy. Being . . . Christophine.

She felt an actually spiritual weariness as she entered the bungalow.

A blaze of sunshine from the window walls, dazzling

powdery, confused her senses. But she took three or four steps away from the elevator at the room's center, and realized that sun and spirit alone were not responsible. Her ears sang insidiously to her; her lungs stopped. She stumbled another step and fell to her knees.

"No, Claudio," she said aloud, to the mote-powdered air, the room with its civilized coffee shadings, the emptiness. Her voice was charged with rage. *"No."*

Her eyes shut.

She lay on the floor, hating him, hating him, a lullaby of hate and love, how she loved the touch of his hands and how lovely it was to go to sleep on the warm cushion-floor with the scent of her own freshly shampooed blue-black hair close about her face. Face it, Magdala, there isn't any way out—out there a real tree moving in the wind—

The drug he must have fed into the veins of her true body in the capsule wiped her brain gently clean with a furry coffee-color floating fist.

But just before she submerged, there came a bright scintilla of thoughts: *I might have been in Two Unit when he did that. Or does he know where I am? Has he somehow kept track of me all this time—sight and sound? Tracked me, but not told me he could. And why do this now? Simply experimenting?*

She woke up in blackness. It did not seem to matter. Then it mattered a great deal.

She struggled to her feet. She did not feel sluggish and had no occasion to. This pseudo flesh she was oriented in was not itself suffering the aftermath of any drug.

Why were there no lights? One subtle light had, she remembered, automatically activated in the bungalow at a night-time human presence.

Her hand brushed through something rustling, papery, yet sinuously humid. She looked at the ceiling, and

saw, through the domed glazium, a black sky patterned
with large white stars which here and there became
wine-red or olive-green behind petals of stained crystal.

She was in the solarium, atop the bungalow and noc-
turnally darkened for the benefit of the plants which
towered around her. But it was not utterly black, the
stars were shining dully on the bronze elevator head in
the middle of the room.

Awake, she had not come to the solarium. Somebody
had brought her there. Only Claudio would want to en-
gineer events in such a way. To ensure that alarm was
grafted upon alarm.

Did he require any other impetus?

She hesitated. Was Claudio still in the bungalow?

She did not, in any case, know which of the multiplic-
ity of buttons on the panel would summon the elevator.

Presently, she pressed a knob at random, and it began
to rain in the solarium. With a strange tin-foil noise, the
plants stirred, advancing their leaves to the water. Magdala stood in the rain, intimidated and profoundly afraid,
as if the induced weather and reciprocal noises of the foliage were sinister token of other irremediable threats.

Finally, she stabbed at the knob once more, and the
rain ceased. She tried a second button with reckless
anxiety, for everything had taken on an aspect of dream-
like derangement.

And sure enough, the result was aptly deranged. The
underfoot paving of the solarium dissipated, and Magdala was rootless in the air, three and a half meters
above the floor of the bungalow.

Her deductive process reassured her instantly. The
paving of the solarium was merely another reversible
window that could be rendered transparent, offering, as
a bird's eye panorama, the apartment below. Her senses
were not, however, able to accept this deduced fact for
some moments.

The bronze shaft of the elevator passed straight downward beneath her into the lower room. Apart from the overhead screening of the bathroom unit, everything else could be seen, even by the yellow crepuscule of the solitary lamp burning in the bungalow. Suspended couch-bed, pneumatic loungers, contrachorda at its northern window-wall. The glazium chimney, spangled with its cherry un-fire, another source of dim illumination. The kitchen space was also to be seen, the beautiful units, the culinary apparatus, the rack of archaic knives.

One knife lay on the floor where she had dropped it. Beside the knife, the dress she had cut in two portions.

She became aware, then, of the other things, as if through the medium of the dress. Somehow, she had not noted them before, as if their incongruity had made them invisible. Or perhaps she had not wanted to see.

To see the additional dresses lying shredded in an oddly structured almost ornamental trail between the kitchen and the raised closet. To see a broken vase, splintered against the mahogany stem of the contrachorda. To see the bolsters disemboweled of their golden embroidery birds. One of the pneumatics had been melodramatically stabbed. Its entrails, too, spilled on the ground.

While she had lain unconscious, Claudio had returned, had taken up his own chosen knife, and loosed his own frenzy with it. She recalled the night at Sugar Beach when he had searched her hotel room for the micro-recorder—the slashed coverings, the deflated chairs.

She recollected hanging from the window, sixty meters above the beach, in his arms.

He was mad, and she had known it almost from the beginning. But why this thing, this foolhardy daylight re-crossing of the island, this ecstasy of ripping and rending that seemed to have been inspired by her own isolated (but also insane?) action with the knife.

Share it with me, he had said. *My hate for Christophine.*

She understood quite suddenly. And, in the second of understanding, the ultimate confirmation came from the night and the holostetic forest.

The soft roar of a car, and the roar dying.

And a little pause.

Down in the garage, where Claudio had left the elevator at his departure, doors opened with an infinitesimal hum. She might have imagined it.

But not the whisper of the car as it drove forward and shut itself off. Not the whisper of the elevator as it flew up into the bungalow.

Not the crisp tap of Christophine's first footfall.

III

THIS WAS THE core of the nightmare.

To lie, body and face pressed to a transparent dense nothing, staring downward. Severed from reality, yet hopelessly snared in it. As yet unfound, unknown. But vulnerable, accessible. To be reached in five seconds by the ascending elevator. And nowhere to hide. No method of evasion.

And mesmerized. Transfixed.

Look in the mirror. The mirror image assumes an actuality of its own. It emerges from the mirror. It lives.

Below, in the crystalline tank, the sumptuous fish swam through its world, thinking itself unique.

Magdala panted as she lay on the dense transparent nothing. She gripped at the nothing with her hands. All over her she was aware of Christophine's lingerie, her woolen dress, her shoes. And by her cheek, heavy silk, grown from her skull, Christophine's hair. And looking through their lids, *Christophine's eyes*.

Christophine del Jan, entering the bungalow, had paused. Seen as she was from above, she was undisclosed, save by stance and gesture. The pause demonstrated that she had noted immediately the wreckage in the room. Yet somehow the lines of her, as she began to move again, did not suggest fear; not even surprise.

She walked directly to the kitchen area, stepping lightly and accurately, without fuss, over the torn garments. The navy blue head was turned. She examined the kitchen, and came out. The bathroom was next.

Christophine was searching for the intruder.

. . . I sent her a stelex. Claudio . . . is in Saint Azoro.

Presumably she had gone to trace him, as Claudio had said. Not succeeding, she had come back. And now, could she tell this was the work of Claudio? Claudio, the only enemy who could break in at the locked door and leave his claw marks within, disappearing like smoke—for he was gone. She had checked the bathroom. She had checked everywhere, and now stood for a moment, motionless.

Her body gave no sign. She did not glance upward. But she must think of the solarium.

Magdala had not yet seen into her face. The foreshortened frame was threatening, but the face—the face was the last terrible fragment of the nightmare. While Christophine did not raise her head, Magdala could endure. She could pretend, if she wished, that Christophine had the face of someone else.

Christophine began to walk, leisurely, meditatively, toward the elevator shaft.

Christophine walked into the cage, out of sight.

Magdala waited for the whisper of the elevator, rising. She could not unglue herself, however, from the floor of the solarium. She did not believe the plants could conceal her. They were Christophine's plants.

She lay plastered to the paving, which had already dried itself after the rain, lay like a rug for Christophine to tread on. If Magdala kept her head pressed to the paving, her eyes tight shut—Christophine might drop dead before she reached her. Or Indigo might revolve from its orbit. Too late. Christophine remained the original. Alpha. Omega.

The whisper of the elevator did not come. Instead, Christophine reappeared from the shaft. This time she carried a traveling bag, which she placed by the raised closet near the bed. With a leisured slovenliness, she began to remove her clothing, letting it fall on to the ground, just as the torn dress, bolsters, vase, had been allowed to fall.

Naked, a blur of warm whiteness, she opened the bag and drew out a lounge robe of maroon velvon, scattering other items as willfully as her clothes.

Pressing together the edges of the robe, she touched the button panel next to the south wall. The closet did not sink, but a polarized bubble arose, packed with bottles and goblets. Christophine poured herself a drink. She tilted her head slightly, stylized, as she drank, but not enough so that Magdala could really see her.

The goblet was like the glassware belonging to Claudio, expensive and fragile, as the broken vase had been.

And with an easy nonchalant swing, Christophine tossed the glass against the southern window-wall, and the glass smashed.

The performance was explicit and effective: Destruction of any sort leaves me unscathed. For I too can destroy.

The man-made bones in Magdala's spine clicked together as a frantic wincing ran down the whole length of her.

Still stretched on the solarium paving, she watched Christophine move to the contrachorda, button lift the lids and the section of strings, and operate the tuning device.

Far off as bells beneath the earth, the notes of the instrument, birthed, failing, born again.

Soon, Christophine, in her maroon robe, seated herself before the contrachorda and began to play.

Curiously, she played music which Magdala knew. Sadrés' "Variations on a Theme by Prokofiev" pierced up through the ceiling-floor like silver wires and thin crystalline rods. They sewed into the solarium, sewed in and out of Magdala's ears and womb. The plants seemed to tremble as the fine needles went through and through them, magically not scoring their leaves. A web of percussion was spun from wall to wall. And Magdala, the fly caught in the web, rather than paralysis, felt herself impelled to get to her feet.

She arrived at the elevator head, tranced, and pushed the third button on the panel.

Christophine went on playing, her back to the shaft.

She expected Claudio. She was spinning the music for Claudio.

Magdala was in the falling elevator.

Five seconds later, she was deposited inside the octagon.

Above, the ceiling was an opaque cobalt lid over the one-way seeing eye of the solarium. Across the wide space, Christophine at the contrachorda, back turned, faceless, playing even now.

Then through the surge and pulse of the music, Christophine spoke.

"Did you reckon on shocking me? I'm not very shockable, my dear. You should know. I checked out the stelex because I like to be thorough, but I never thought I'd find you that way. It had to be something like this—childish, with the cunning and inventiveness of a child. I'll admit, I'm intrigued as to how you got through the security checkposts without a current print and voice-match. Some gadget? Always so amazing with the gadget. But, yes, you have been rather wonderful. You have everything on the boil.

But really, Claudio, you can't expect to have me on the boil, too."

And merging upward, shadow upon shadow, from the keyboard, Christophine reversed herself to confront the threshold of the elevator shaft.

Magdala stood, as if vitrified, the onslaught already upon her in the fraction of a second before it occurred, already preparing her, embalming her. Verity was no more frightful than her dread had forecast.

But for Christophine, apparently, no forecast had been accomplished, despite her words.

It was not that she did anything, said anything. In fact, it was as if she came to a standstill inside herself, and everything lifelike seemed to slide away. She had been changed to some brittle frosted substance. A breath, and she might shatter, like her glass.

The iridescent blue neon eyes did not blink, because a blink would fracture them, and shards of sapphire would sprinkle the floor.

I'm the real one, Magdala thought, but the thought made her shudder.

Then Christophine drew in her breath. And did not break.

"You're not a holostet, I can see that. You must be the real thing. The genuine article. Where does it say it? Is it stamped between your breasts? Where does it say: *Claudio Loro built me*?"

Magdala felt her awareness of identity pass. Everything passed. The world passed. All that was left was Christophine.

Six

In the Forests of the Night

I

"AND WHERE IS HE?"
Magdala did not answer.

Christophine had faultlessly re-assembled herself. Unnecessarily, cogently, she elaborated. "I refer to Claudio. Where is Claudio?"

"Somewhere on the island."

"You can do better than that."

"I can't." It would not hurt Magdala to betray the hated man, but she could not, for in this too, he had left her in ignorance. Which decreed she must instead frustrate the hated woman.

Hate Christophine. Did Magdala hate her? Magdala became conscious that her face had borrowed the frigid and ordered rictus of Christophine's—while Christophine's gestures were being reflexively communicated to her own shoulders, fingers, torso.

She could not take her eyes off Christophine. Christophine dominated her vision. Everything. The angle of the head, the slender muscles flickering in her arms as she moved her hands. The white neck, pollen-dusted by its freckles, the hair, the leaf blue irises. To copy was inevitable. It was a mirror. It was herself. Now she could see it all as it truly was.

"And your actual body," Christophine said casually and appositely, in Magdala's own voice, "where is that?"

It was difficult to believe there was another body. It always had been difficult.

"With Claudio," Magdala said. It did not really trouble her now. It was like being asked where she had put her purse, or her jacket.

"I see. A hostage. He doesn't trust you completely then. Why not?"

Magdala stood in silence, watching Christophine. Watching how the waves of hair lay level on the shoulders of the maroon robe, but shifting, one by one, a sea at night.

"Yes," Christophine said. Her tone was harsh. "It's fascinating, isn't it? One should feel threatened, but somehow one does not. Sublimation, perhaps? Yet no fear. That's odd. Maybe Claudio knew it would be this way. But this way is more treacherous than any other. So tell me. Why did you agree to it?"

"Agree?" Magdala spoke deliberately, exactly as Christophine finished speaking. The voices seemed to overlap. The same voice, blending.

"Agree to jettison your own identity and take on mine? Astrads?"

"No." Magdala placed the word once more directly against Christophine's last word. An echo effect. Was that what made it so pleasing?

"Don't do that," Christophine said.

"What?"

"That. Fitting what you say to anchor the periods of my sentences. It's probably instinctive, but Claudio would delight in it. I suspect Claudio of re-inventing the Narcissus principle for my benefit. Yes, that makes sense. He would think me capable of that. Don't say 'Narcissus?'"

An Earth-european myth. An unusually attractive boy saw his reflection in a pool. He lay down and stared at the reflection, unable to look away. He never looked away again. Generally interpreted as an allegory of homosexual love, or a vulgar illustration of ego-mania. Why am I talking so much? Of course. I feel I know you. I do know you. But you haven't answered my question. Pause before you say 'What question?' Don't anchor me again."

Magdala paused. She said, "I remember the question."

Christophine suddenly walked forward.

Magdala found she had automatically copied the action. With about half a meter between them, Christophine stopped, and Magdala stopped. With no warning, and no prologue, Christophine struck her across the cheek, a biting, accurate blow. (Claudio had struck her.)

"That is for your pretty impersonation of me," Christophine said, but her face was expressionless. "I can't imagine how he persuaded you. I don't really care very much. He was handsome and he was rich. One or the other, or both, got to you. But did he explain *why*?"

Magdala paused as she had been requested to do, and her face stung like bruised human flesh.

"Hatred," she said eventually.

"Because of what?"

"He never told me."

"Then I'll tell you."

Christophine pushed her, and Magdala fell backward into one of the uninjured pneumatics. (This far, Christophine had made no comment on the torn room, the shredded clothing, dismissing them presumably as Claudio's malevolence, or Magdala's in the capacity of Claudio's robot.)

Christophine did not sit. Her strategy was plain and admirable. She had deployed a fundamental difference in posture between them, to offset their hypnotic sameness. Other deployments followed. She took a long blue cigarette from a box beside the drinks bubble. Systematically she shut the box, drew on the cigarette to light it.

As she talked, smoking the cigarette in rapid breathless drags that carried the inhalation no deeper than her throat, she also paced, tiger-like, the whole length of the room and back again.

"Claudio and I," said Christophine, her words visible as silver smoke, "had a flying start in life. We were born glamorous and rich. One helps the other, you see. Not just a good cheap genetic pre-conception match. A privately paid-for delineated match. Leading to children with exceptional looks and exceptional brains. Coupled to wealth, who would lose? Claudio lost. He grew up and acquired another thing. Eccentricity. You would like to hear where we met? Naturally you would. We met here, at Marine Bleu, which is where the whole C. T. Project was begun. Conjure up an image of us. Two talented pretty people in a monochrome landscape. We were magnetized. We touch. Let me unveil Claudio Loro, the mysterious genius. Claudio Loro is so rich he never had to work at anything. Science was—is—his pastime. His only motive in becoming a scientist has been to stave off boredom. When we met, he had many more astrads than I. That was all right. He could be magnanimous and kind to me. He could give me things. Then he found out that not only did he have more astrads, he had a few less brains. Are you able to accept that? No. How can you? Claudio's the most brilliant, most dynamic, most exotic creature you've ever come across. Even for me. It took me two years of the C. T. Project with Claudio, and two years of bed with Claudio and fights with Claudio, to realize. Beautiful Claudio hates what is superior to beautiful Claudio. While he is just a little more rich, a little more beautiful, a little more clever, he will love you. He hates me. I accept that. It's logical. I am too clever for Claudio.

"I mentioned the C. T. Project. C.T. stands for Consciousness Transferal—the thing Claudio has achieved with you. What Two Unit has been struggling to achieve for ten years. What I have been personally struggling with for three years. Did Claudio inveigle you into Two Unit? I think that he did. Then you'll have seen the mess we're in. Emilion—I can judge from your face. Emilion's dead, is he? I won't waste time on comments. He is another heir to the long line of potential mishaps and heartbreaks. By which you know we've failed. We have no apparent excuse. From the start, we've had full E.C. backing. Of course, the advantages of Consciousness Transferal are sufficiently blatant that Earth Conclave had no choice. A score of out-Conclave planets might have picked up our line otherwise, and financed us. Initially, C.T. looked set to be a winner. Five years: that was the estimate for a breakthrough. And a breakthrough was urgent. Spare-parting and implant medication have been at a terminus for a century. The rejection factor has never been adequately solved. Plastic surgery and its adjunct, bionics, tend to degenerate. Even successes are tied to a hospital routine. There's no mechanical replacement that can institute a totally normal life-style. C.T. solves all of that. Any whole brain can be aphysically salvaged from any damaged body. No surgery is necessary, no hospitalization is necessary. Capsule care is the only linking factor. Otherwise, the C.T. beneficiary is free, and in a superior physical condition to that of the average human subject. I'm lecturing you, incidentally, because I doubt if Claudio bothered to detail any of the vital intention of this struggle of ours. He's used the ideology of Two Unit as a backdrop for his own warped and theatrical passions. Just as he's used you. As he'd like to use me. No, as he has used me."

II

CHRISTOPHINE HAD CONCLUDED her pacing. She stood at the northeastern window. She seemed to be looking out at the soulless perpendiculars of the forest.

"One night," said Christophine to the forest beyond the window, "Claudio and I were working alone in the computer lab here at Bleu. It was nearly midnight. We were no longer lovers, he and I, and barely colleagues. But a certain equation had been fed to the computer at twenty-four o'clock, and certain surprising results were coming out. We stayed there in that white-lit room, drinking coffee from plastic beakers, not talking, waiting. And then the computer produced the answer. The computer is God. You resent it, but you worship. God has the last word. This last word was what Two Unit had been praying for. It was the rundown by which C.T. could be achieved. You understand, I'm giving you nothing technical, nothing you can't grasp. That's important. I want you to know, Narcissa, just what you've gotten yourself involved in.

"The result was the computer's. But the stimuli, the qualified data which produced the result—these were mine. Not Claudio's. Mine. Can you imagine what that would do to Claudio? You must know him, to some extent. You must have learned that everything must progress according to the laws which Claudio stipulates.

"Does Claudio seem to you unbalanced? Even demented? That night Claudio was out of his mind."

Christophine turned from the window, glowing against it, gazing at Magdala.

"Claudio went to the console. He snapped the plastase strip from the channel, coiled it, and put it in the zip pocket of his coat. While he did so, he blocked off the screen of the console from me. Then, he leaned sideways and did something to the panel-bank. Claudio was always astute with machinery. There wasn't a sec-lock in the building he couldn't override. And now he overrode the computer. There is a key to erase superfluous experimentation, but the computer will analyze whatever it's asked to erase, and, in the event of error, will retain the material. Claudio somehow bypassed the analysis system. He coerced the computer into a position where it erased not only the result of the data, but the data itself. No tabular records had been kept, except by sonogram, which had been stored in the computer itself. When Claudio pressed the key, everything went. Months of calculation, days of computation. The answer. And Claudio leaned there, the snapped-off plastase that represented the answer in his pocket. He grinned and said, 'Now, shall I swallow it?' You can envisage him, can't you, saying that. Just then one of the leads from the panel-bank shorted out. Claudio's override had a dramatic bonus. I'm sure it thrilled him, sparks and fire going up all around his Lucifer party-piece. I ran to the console and hit the emergency button, and in twenty seconds more the sprinklers were on. By then, Claudio had gone. I thought it was another crazy game of his, but it wasn't. He headed for the north-side jet sheds. He stole an auto-aqua, reprogrammed it, and got over to the mainland with his car in the storage bay. Bleu security never stopped him. Two things that never stop Claudio—machines and conscience. We got the jet back, but not Claudio. I assume he drove the car out of the jet bay and kept on driving, until he arrived somewhere he wanted to be. He had nothing with him—clothing, rare books from Earth, paintings— everything was left behind in his apartment on the station. He only took the car and the plastase strip in his pocket."

Christophine dropped her cigarette into a bronze-beaked disposer near the window. Her face seemed to swim in the darkness at her back; she looked withdrawn and disciplined to a point of inhumanity.

"I didn't reveal what he had done," she said unemphatically. "Can you credit that? Yes, obviously you can. To run out on E. C. Research was a dangerous enough thing for him to do. If they'd known he had the key to the Two Unit C. T. Project in his pocket when he ran, they would have hounded him like a plague rat. So I said nothing. They thought the computer had malfunctioned spontaneously. I didn't tell them what had gone before. With that much data lost, no one was amazed at Claudio's desertion, or that the project itself was put back five months.

"I thought," Christophine said, "he'd use what he'd got. Any moment I expected the news to explode. From some out-Conclave planet, perhaps, or from Claudio in person, claiming mastery in the field of private research. But it's taken him a long while to unravel the computer's cryptography. Three years. I'd considered he might be dead. Then the Saint Azoro stelex. And then . . . then you. I wonder," Christophine said, "what he means to bring about, this way. Plainly, he wants to frighten me, undermine me. I could never reproduce that former line of data Claudio destroyed. It was one of those inspired accidents of the mind that never came to Claudio. Besides, I've had to preserve the subterfuge that we never got the answer that night, in order to shield him, protect him from an E.C. government witch-hunt. That must make me a fool, I suppose. Just what he always wanted me to be. Is that what he's trying to say, sending me you? What reaction does he anticipate? What is he hoping will happen? He could be watching us, using your transfer body as some sort of relay device. My God, with your internal android structuring, you could be a walking Tri-V set. I hazard you wouldn't have been informed. But no, that can't be the case. Mechanisms at that power level would have activated alarms all over the station. I'll conjecture your body contains some simple contrivance whereby he can ascertain your whereabouts—nothing more."

Magdala was awash in the sea of information Christophine had released to engulf her. Flotsam rose to a swirling surface—the description of Claudio beside the console, the essential plastase strip in his pocket; the idea that she herself might be rigged with mechanized implements for Claudio's convenience. Under and about everything, the duality she shared with Christophine. There was, too, the residue of questions she had not formulated, for example, a question concerning the man Paul Hovak, and what his role might be in this tangle of chiaroscuro, declarations, vitriol.

Christophine watched her drowning.

Christophine said calmly, "Whatever else we differ on, Narcissa, I think you will agree that Claudio has obtained the upper hand. You and I, we're the ones who are lost in the wood."

In the chimney, the un-fire blazed, cherry red. Outside the trees loomed. A wind was blowing through the electric forest.

"Narcissa," said Christophine. She was lighting another cigarette, pouring herself another drink. She offered neither to Magdala. "What is your name, by the way?"

Magdala opened her mouth. As twice before, no voice would come.

"I assure you of this," Christophine said, "you can't

have my name. Whatever Claudio Loro promised you. Perhaps I should call you Claudia. Merely the feminine version of your master."

"Magdala," Magdala said. The regeneration of her voice caught her sharply, like a cough.

"Well, Magdala, have you decided what you want to do? Are you going to make Claudio happy by trying to hurt me?"

Magdala stared at her. Nothing seemed substantial— the fire, the room; and the forest was not substantial. Only Christophine.

"He didn't think you would be here this quickly," Magdala said. She was attempting to convey her own notion that Claudio had, by some as-usual unspecified sciento-mechanic means—monitoring of the checkposts, perhaps?—discerned the instant of Christophine's return. That he had, therefore, rushed to the bungalow and ripped her clothes and furniture, as a last display of malignity. That he had then deserted the island, and Magdala, leaving chaos to work itself out.

"But he did. He would comprehend I could hardly be away long," Christophine corrected her. "He's here on the island, anticipating. He may well believe you will feel sufficiently endangered by my appearance to attack and kill me. Had you considered that?"

"No."

"No. I accept as much. Neither of us, strangely, feels like dueling with the other. That at least is a correct appraisal of myself. You?"

"The same."

"Why not? We are Armageddon to each other, surely?"

"I don't know why not."

"Is it simply that you hate Claudio fractionally more than you are prepared to hate me?"

Magdala shut her eyes. She could not think while the

icon of Christophine was before her. From a vast depth within herself, and from the sea which covered her, she dredged up a name.

"Paul Hovak," Magdala said.

"What?" Without looking at her, Magdala was conscious of Christophine's alertness.

"I wanted to ask you about Paul Hovak."

"Why?"

Rather as Magdala had done earlier, Christophine was synchronizing her retaliatory questions like a drumbeat to hit squarely at the ends of Magdala's sentences. Instinctive on Christophine's part?

"Claudio took me to a hotel on the mainland. Paul Hovak was there. Claudio wanted you to be discredited with Hovak, and I didn't know who Hovak was."

"My God," said Christophine. "Oh, my God."

Magdala raised her lids cautiously, as if against fierce light. Christophine was revealed in profile, body and face. Sculptured, gorgeous, the glass hanging loose from her grip, spilling its liquor on the floor.

"Yes, I see," Christophine said. She let go the glass, and moving about, stepped on it, inadvertently or purposely, Magdala was not sure. Full face now, Christophine came to Magdala. Christophine leaned down into the pneumatic and drew Magdala out of it, upward, toward her, as if to lift her into her arms.

And Christophine was indeed holding her now, like a lover, like Claudio, holding Magdala pressed to her, their eyes, nostrils, mouths a few centimeters apart.

"Hovak," Christophine said. Her breath was sweet, lightly glazed with alcohol and smoke. The scent of her skin and hair was the scent of Magdala's skin and hair, no divergence save for the faint amber-color hint of sandalwood. "I must hear everything that occurred between you and Hovak."

Magdala saw herself reflected in the eyes of Christophine. Blue on blue, image upon image, mirror upon mirror.

Christophine blinked, Magdala blinked.

Magdala began to tell Christophine about Paul Hovak. First, the holostet. Next the scene on the pier of Sugar Beach, recognition and unrecognition, Irlin and his text-book blow. Hovak later in the suite, checking the rooms, humorously warning, altering to anger. But while she said all this, she had no positive sense of what she said. Merely of Christophine.

After a time, silence. Magdala had ended her narrative of Paul Hovak.

"And Claudio," Christophine murmured. Her eyes were nearly closed, as Magdala realized her own must again have become.

"Claudio?"

"He would want more than simply to discredit me with Paul. I can rectify that. Claudio understands that I can."

"Claudio recorded our conversation in the suite," Magdala whispered. Standing like this, against Christophine, she felt no excitement, no stress. It was almost as if she were near to sleep. To blissful, dreamless, infinite oblivion. . . .

The hands which were holding her arms bit into her. Hovak had held her this way. And Claudio. Now Christophine. Magdala did not mind that Christophine was hurting her. But spontaneously, Magdala's own hands, acquiescent at her sides before, slid forward and seized in turn the flesh of Christophine. So she felt Christophine's sudden fear pass, as if by osmosis of their tissue and blood, into her own self.

"Why did he record your conversation?" Christophine said. "He could have listened through the device by relay, heard what Paul said to you directly. Why record? Christ. I know why. Magdala," Christophine said, "Magdala."

Her face drained white as a stone beside a beach, its pale gold fleckings growing dark and livid on the whiteness. Magdala felt herself emulating, blanching, a slow sickening wave of blood abandoning her head. "Listen," said Christophine, "would you like to destroy me? Claudio would. He isn't content with what he did to me before. He wants my bones. But you. How about you?"

"I—don't want to harm you."

"No?"

"No. No."

"Because I can tell you something now that would assist you to crucify me. Assist Claudio to crucify me. Would you like to?"

"No, Christophine."

"Listen, then. Paul and I are connected in this way. We plan to sell the data for the C. T. Project off-planet, outside of Earth Conclave. It isn't as bad as it sounds. We feel that once Consciousness Transferral has been solved, the method should be available to all planetary Federations, not simply within E.C. Peace, for example, with its unstable volcanic zones, has a high rate of crippling accidents. Are we expected to leave people without hope of a conclusive painless salvation simply because—but no, no politics. You accept what I mean."

Magdala nodded. But she nodded because Christophine burned before her, her fires seeping in through Magdala's pores, consuming heart and brain.

"But," Christophine said, "if E.C. learns what Paul and I mean to promote, we're finished. In all ways, finished. Claudio knows. He will do this: He will use the recording of Paul's conversation with you to make a simulate voice which will register on any machine that checks it, as Paul's natural voice—there is no other method of successfully faking a voice save by simulate. Gadgetry genius again, you see. Claudio will then signal Marine Bleu. He will ensure that the signal seems to originate as a call from the mainland. Claudio will use Paul's simulate-voice in the signal. The sim-voice will disclose our plans. How will it go? Something like this: 'Christophine del Jan has double-crossed me. She has already sold the secrets of C.T. out-Conclave, cutting me out of the deal. Thus, vengefully, I betray her to you.' That will settle both of us. I will be arrested. The machines will trace Paul and he will be arrested. Our activities will be uncovered swiftly. We'll be shipped back to Earth to face a Traitor's Tribunal. God help us."

"Claudio has no machinery with him," Magdala said. "If he's on the island, how can he—"

"He has the big car, I suppose—does he? The car contains chassis-storage. There would be room for all he would need in that, and to spare. Don't underestimate him. He didn't even tell you where he would be. If only he had told you."

They stood together, breathing each other in, softly.

But I know where he is, Magdala suddenly thought. *There is only one place he would go to ground.* She was amazed Christophine could not see it too. On this island, all rock and cement, cloaked by holostets, otherwise naked. How was it Christophine had not guessed?

She could give Christophine this gift of Claudio.

Should she?

Why not. Claudio was the enemy.

Christophine was—was—

"Christophine," Magdala said. "Claudio and the car. They're on the north side of the island. In one of the caves at the foot of the cliff."

Christophine had pulled the traveling bag wide. She had removed from it a dust pink dress and handed the dress to Magdala.

"Put this on. Claudio has an eye for detail. He saw

what was in the closet. It should be a garment he didn't spot. One I must have brought with me. Proof of the homecoming."

Magdala had taken off the white dress, donned the dust pink dress.

Christophine watched her, but Magdala was not unnerved by this. And suddenly Christophine quoted at her, musingly, something that was vaguely familiar, something purely apposite, and it seemed to lift both of them into another sphere, their condition honored and immanent. "The one so like the other as could not be distinguished but by names."

When Magdala was re-dressed (there was a note of sandalwood in the fabric), Christophine discarded her velvon robe, took up the white zipless, still warm from Magdala, and put it on. "It seems applicable. Do you agree? The closet's single un-knifed dress."

I slashed with a knife also, Magdala thought. But it was foolish and laughable to think of that.

Then Christophine offered her a drink. Christophine did not comment on the fact that the drink, in Magdala's case, would be superfluous. She offered in courtesy, as if to a whole and human woman. They drank together. It sealed, without words, their pact.

The course to be followed was straightforward.

They would drive together back along the road to the north side of the island. The tables would be exquisitely turned. Claudio's scenario pre-empted.

Their preparations, the exchange of garments, the symbolic drink, occupied brief minutes. The total sequence they had shared had not lasted long. And yet, was timeless.

Before they left the bungalow, Christophine had called Two Unit, utilizing, as off-handedly as Claudio, a code.

Presently, Doramel had manifested herself in the vision plate.

Christophine said:

"How did Val manage with Emilion's autopsy? Find anything?"

"Nothing out of the ordinary, M. del Jan. I'm sorry."

"Don't be. Any calls?"

"No, M. del Jan."

"All right, Doramel. Goodnight."

"Goodnight, M. del Jan," said neat dark Doramel.

Christophine came from the panel. She laid one hand gently upon Magdala's shoulder.

"So far, so good. Claudio believes he has unlimited space to indulge in cat and mouse, but he hasn't. I can stop him from making that call, with your help. You won't fail me?"

"No."

"And afterwards—" Christophine said.

Quietly, Magdala said:

"You have me. The first success of Transfer. You can study me, learn Claudio's secret."

"Not if it would distress you."

"How could it?"

Magdala wanted to say something else. She wanted to say *I love you*. Not sexual love, not even love, perhaps. A special, unheard-of foreign thing, marvelous, pervasive. But there was no necessity to express this verbally. Her eyes expressed it, her body.

She had never been able to come close to anything before. She and Claudio had clashed glancingly in shadow and raw glare. But now, finally, to touch and to be touched. Not physically but with the soul.

I would die for her. It can't matter if I die, while she lives. We're indivisible. One.

In Christophine's car, Christophine gave her, unspeaking, a miniature delectro. Ivory was inlaid beside the barrel. It was like the delectro in the Tri-V drama at Sugar Beach when the rich man shot himself.

III

A S EACH BREAKER came in over the rocks,
about once every eleven seconds, there was a sound
like tearing cloth. As if the night itself were being torn
down its black seams, torn open on a further blackness,
from which the white spume gushed like plasma. The
slender concrete promenade between the base of the
cliff and the detonating sea was viscous and shining
from a recent attempt the waves must have made to
overpower the land. Under the cliff, in a line westward
from the fluorescent metal road, the nine caves (they
had now been counted) continued extravagantly to
gape. They were just too high for the invading ocean to
have probed them. Too low for the forest to mask them.
They suggested a hunger for something. Like starving
mouths or obscene wombs, they seemed begging to be
filled.

The woman stood thirteen meters from the road and
from the closed car. She was roughly level with the
rocky slope which led into the fifth cave, the middle
cave. The wind from the sea, tepid, omnipresent, and
saline, struck against her hair, the material of her rose-
beige frock. Only the open zip pocket of the frock did

not respond to the wind. The pocket was weighted, and immovable.

The woman had stood there in the loud night, before the fifth cave, for forty-one seconds.

Between the breakers, there was always a hesitation of spurling half-silence. In the lull that came at the forty-seventh second, the woman shouted:

"Claudio! I killed her, Claudio!"

Another breaker interrupted at this point. When the lull resumed, around the sixty-fourth second, the woman shouted again.

"I killed her. Claudio! I killed Christophine."

The seventy-fifth second, the breaker. The eighty-first second, the lull:

"Claudio! I'm wearing Christophine's dress. I—"

The breaker. The ninety-eighth second, the lull:

"I knifed her, Claudio. The blood went all—"

The breaker. The hundred and fifteenth second, the lull:

"The blood, Claudio. All over my white dress."

The breaker. The one hundred and thirty-third second, the lull:

"So I took a dress from her bag, Claudio. Come and see—"

The breaker. The hundred and forty-ninth second, the lull.

"Come and look at me, Claudio! I killed Christophine!"

The hundred and sixtieth second: the breaker.

Claudio walked out of the seventh cave, to her left.

He wore black; black trousers, black shirt. She might not have seen him but for the pallor of neck and hands and face, the extreme pallor of the hair. His face was bland, which meant that her voice, shouting through the night and the sea, had startled him and the startlement needed to be masked.

He did not shout back at her. He did not approach any nearer.

"Come here," she called in the next lull.

The breakers crashed, ebbed, crashed. At last, not answering her, he began to walk toward her down the rock.

Claudio. He had been himself with both of them, both Christophine and Magdala. He had twisted them and played with them, sneered, damaged, put them to use. But she did not have to have this sisterhood of hate with Christophine to strengthen her. She did not even hate Claudio any more. She did not require the weapon of hate against him. Indifference made her invulnerable. Christophine made her invulnerable.

He was on the concrete promenade, and she could see him better. His mouth was white as his face. His eyes, the pupils dilated, were black as his shirt. He had now advanced sufficiently near. As if he knew that, he stopped.

"You killed Christophine," he said.

She dropped her hand into her pocket, withdrew it, the delectro ready clasped, slipping the gauge along its counter as she did so.

"Actually, no."

He swallowed; the undulation of his throat was well defined, almost convulsive.

But—"Ah," he said, most musically, as if he sang, "I should have foreseen this, shouldn't I?"

To her right, thirteen meters away, she heard the side of Christophine's car rising.

Claudio did not turn to look. He looked only at Magdala.

"Don't," he said, "let her get into the cave."

Magdala made an "O" of her mouth, raised her eyebrows, popped her eyes, miming the astounded puppet, as once Claudio had done, with her.

"I mean it," he said.

"I'm sure you do."

"Christ. You even sound like her."

"Well, I should, shouldn't I? That was what you wanted."

He took a couple of strides forward and she raised the barrel of the delectro.

"You've never fired one of those things," he said.

"No. But at this range, I can hardly miss, can I?"

"Magda—" he said. He stuttered slightly. "Magda—there's a reason she mustn't go into the cave—"

"Of course there is. Your car is there. And the machinery packed up in the chassis-storage—compartments you never showed me. And the simulate of Paul's voice. You haven't had a chance to use that yet. You delayed for the crowd, an audience tomorrow. Stupid, Claudio. You're stupid."

"Yes, if you like. Anything. But Magdala, you have to prevent Christophine from reaching the cave."

At that moment, Christophine moved across the rock behind Claudio. Watching Claudio carefully, Magdala saw merely the white blur of Christophine's dress at the corner of her eye. But something at the center of her emotions, her very life, paeaned, vibrated, glittered.

"Is she there yet?" Claudio asked. "Tell me, Magdala—"

The white blur melted in the black mouth of the seventh cave.

"Yes," Magdala said.

He sighed. Suddenly he reached out and took her face in his hands. The delectro pressed into him. He ignored it.

His touch was as she remembered. His beautiful, magical, magician's touch. But it no longer had any importance. Lust, joy, agony—dregs of the mind. He could stir her, but not hypnotize her—not now.

"It isn't Paul's simulate voice she wants," said Claudio

softly. "It's you and me she wants, dead. You couldn't bring yourself to kill her, but she'll kill you with impunity."

"Oh, no," Magdala said. She smiled. She even shifted the delectro slightly, to make him more comfortable as he leaned toward her, she was that indifferent.

"Yes, Magda. Yes, she can. What story did she offer you? I can imagine. But don't forget what's in the left side of the chassis-storage. Your capsule. Do you think she isn't aware of that?"

Before she could assimilate his actions, his hands darted from her face and snapped shut about her fingers. Simultaneously he jerked aside, wrenching the delectro from her grip. And in the same instant, automatically, she fired.

Claudio uttered the oddest sound, without timbre, isolated and quite unidentifiable as human. The energy bolt had thrown him, but not far. He landed on the concrete, rolling, curling, uncurling. His right hand contained the delectro, held by the barrel. His left hand flapped, the bones smashed. He gave the sound again, and it was exactly as before, unresonant, like wood striking on wood. He curled together, uncurled, curled, and the delectro dropped out of his right hand. He seemed to try to recapture it. It met his legs as he rolled, shot away, and fell over the promenade into the sea.

Magdala felt a wave of giddiness. The sea, the cliff, the concrete all swung in a huge arc and settled with nauseating abruptness.

And then Christophine had re-appeared in the mouth of the cave. She emerged like a spirit from hell, lifting one arm. She held a piece of a machine under the other, a metal plaque of dead lights, trailing wires.

"*Good*!" she cried across the night, across the breakers, and Magdala heard her. "Good, Magdala. Clever, clever." Christophine shone whitely. She was a star. She ran down the rock. "Stay there, watch him. Just let me start the car—"

Somehow, Magdala had lost her. Already lost. Magdala saw her run to the car, throw in the mechanical thing, step in after it. Magdala saw the side of the car shut, and heard the motor roar.

Christophine's car sped up the metal road into the forest.

Magdala stood alone but not surprised. Empty, of course.

Each time the lull came, she heard Claudio make the wooden noise. She understood he was attempting to drag himself along the rock slope, back into the cave.

Across the sea, there came a pang of thunder.

Empty.

Empty.

IV

AFTER SOME WHILE, perhaps three-quarters of an hour, Magdala began to walk along the slope toward the cave, following Claudio. She felt a leaden curiosity as to what had become of him. Reiterating ceaselessly that ghastly wooden grunt of pain, he had gradually hauled himself into the cave, out of sight. And the cave, distance, the sea, had extinguished any further sounds he might or might not have made.

The cave smelled stagnant, smelled of blackness. Though deep in the pit of it a sour light soaked through the black, which was the faint glow of a car headlamp. Claudio's car lay in the cave, a sea beast, a large silver fish, stranded by a great penetrating retreating wave. Entering, she could only discern the face of it, with no sign of Claudio there, but the left-hand side sections of the car, back and front, were raised. As she went forward and drew level with them, she beheld Claudio, silent now, and slumped across the front seat. His head hung from his neck rather as the broken hand hung from his wrist, as if his neck were broken, too. But he glanced up at her.

"Just a minute," he said tonelessly. "Not that I don't

think you should see what she did. Yes, I think you deserve that. But not quite yet."

She halted, gazing at him wildly. It was not that she had forgotten Christophine's theft from the car, the plaque of dead lights under her arm. But all that Christophine meant to Magdala now had been reduced to a cleaving in twain: the emptiness.

"You gulped down the story that she wanted Hovak's simulate voice tape," he said. "Didn't you realize that what she took from here wasn't anything like that? I'll tell you what it was. It was a panel ripped out of the side of a maintenance capsule. That's just the very thing she was desperate to get. The panel carries the energy charge during Transfer—you remember? Never mind. Like any good piece of mechanics, the panel has a data bank. All she need do now is plug it into the computer at Two Unit and the computer will analyze the data. In about ten hours, she'll have the answer to C.T. She'll be able to transfer the consciousness of any man or woman she chooses into any simulate body she chooses, with a success rate of ninety-nine point nine percent."

Claudio eased his position slightly, lolling his head lethargically to let it rest against the seat.

"I'm tired," he said. "I can't decide if it's better to explain first, or let you see first, then explain. Whatever I do, there isn't much time to do it in."

Outside, the thunder split the night. An antiseptic lightning smacked against the sea.

"Damn you," she murmured. "Do you think I'll always comply with everything you say?"

He yawned, and then to her horror, he started to cry.

The tears spilled out under his lashes in two narrow streams. He did not seem aware of them, but they filled her with an impulse to violence. Desperately, she flung herself around the car to the rear.

The entire chassis-storage, three compartments in

all, had been opened and withdrawn. Her maintenance capsule was the first thing before her and she almost fell over it. Her hands on the glazium, she stared at the monster inside, wrapped in its cocoon. Nothing appeared to be wrong. Then she noticed that the wires leading into the drip-feed were not whole, but, having been broken, had been resealed on the breaks. Nor was her foot unbalanced by an uneven pebble. She moved her foot and looked down and saw a plastic syringe containing a third its length of greenish fluid.

She must have made a sound. She heard him call her name from inside the car.

"It's all right," he said to her. "It's toxic, but it didn't get very far into your system before I closed the drip. It was a botched job, for Christophine. But, of course, she had other things on her mind."

Magdala was bowed over the glazium capsule, clutching it, supported by it. She recollected the swirl of giddiness and nausea. Christophine. Christophine had intended to kill her after all.

And then she felt the panel set in the side of her capsule, whole and attached beneath her palm. And then she lifted her eyes and looked across at the right hand storage area, pulled with the rest of the compartments onto the floor of the cave.

"Claudio," she said, "Claudio, Claudio, Claudio."

He said: "You've seen. Now come here."

"Claudio," she said. She wanted to laugh, but no laugh was available. Instead, she found she was crying, too, and blinkered now by tears instead of desperation, she obeyed him.

His own display of grief or pain or weakness was ended. He had maneuvered himself again, along the seat, providing room for her to crawl into the car beside him.

"Isn't it fantastic," he said. "We can cry. Don't you

think that's fantastic, Magdala? Like real people. In the beginning, I never knew it could happen. But Magdala, cry sotto voce. Listen to me. I've got about five minutes, that's all."

Her tears were dry. She sat beside him, her eyes fixed on him, her ears listening. The world had shrunk to fit into her eyes, her ears. Outside, chaos roiled.

Lightning was striking the forest, repeatedly. A thousand colors reflected on the breakers of the sea, the black wall of the night, poured over into the cave, the car. Yellow, lilac, carmine; purple, turquoise, green. The shades of antique golden coins, of blue fish scales, of dusks, of dawns, of fires and alcohols, stained glass, flowers and blood.

"I don't know what Christophine told you," he had said, "but you're going to hear the truth now. And this version has the advantage of already having been proven to you, by the second maintenance capsule you discovered. The capsule that belongs to me.

"Once upon a time, three years ago, when I was controller of the C. T. Project on Marine Bleu, the beautiful Christophine was assigned as my sub. I have no doubt she hated that, but she was clever enough not to show me how much. What she did show me was her order-built bungalow and the way into her bed. We were near to cracking C.T. That is a fact. Near enough to be excited and to have made provision. The first two guinea pigs for Transfer were going to be Christophine and myself, and to that end the genetic blueprints of both our physical structures had been prepared. Then one night Christophine suggested an extra angle to me. I doubt you're *au fait* with planetary politics, Magdala, but the position is roughly this. Earth Conclave comprises fifty colonized worlds. Outside the Conclave there are around a hundred planets that have broken with Earth and formed their own Federations. There is already a trade war, and what comes next is anybody's guess. The situation is on ice, but a single advantage in any field could swing the balance. C.T. is obviously a medical advantage. But it has a far more interesting viability in the area of espionage. An illustration—a key figure in a trade delegation can be eliminated and replaced by a simulate. The simulate will be indistinguishable from the original. Even prints and voice, the two things that surgery can never fake, would be exact. And inside this simulate is the transferred consciousness of a hand-picked saboteur. With an E.C. research unit within an ace of cracking C.T., the Out-Conclave Federations were getting restive. Accordingly, the rat named Hovak had made a contact with Christophine, and introduced to her the enthralling notion of selling C.T. to the highest bidder, with Hovak himself as well-paid go-between. Wonder why Christa brought this juicy snippet to me? Because she had to. Because if anyone made the breakthrough on C.T., I was going to be the one—not Christa, though I'll swear that isn't her story.

"I made the breakthrough three nights later. I was alone at the Unit. It was a random series, punched up on the computer console. The answer came back in sixty seconds. It was that uncomplex. Too uncomplex.

"There isn't time to tell you what went on in my head, Magda. Maybe when they split the atom, they had a taste of it. Patently not enough of a taste. But for me—the implications, Magda, the misuse, the bloody evil that could be devised. Not only the usual spy network filth. Individuals buying their way in on it, setting it up for private mayhem—I could be right or wrong. I was God in that lab, Magda. For ten whole minutes I was God. Then I acted God, and I overrode the analysis system on the computer and erased the data. Five months' worth of work, the sonograms, the random series. The answer. Gone.

"And then Christophine walked in.

"There was screaming written all over her face, but no scream came out. She'd had a premonition of what I might do. Just too late. It wasn't that she needed the cash. It was the power she needed. She wants to rule the galaxy, Magda. I think I mean that literally. She wants us all to run on rails, with her fingers on the keys. Play us like her contrachorda. And she looks like an angel. A blue-haired angel, Magda. . . .

"'What have you done,' she said. Of course, she knew what I'd done. She knew me very well by then. But I couldn't resist it, Magda, the temptation was too magnificent. I revealed to her, carefully, that I'd destroyed the data so no one else could beat us to our shimmering Out-Conclave sale. There were a couple of reels of plastase, random series with nonsense computations, lying on the desk under the console. Computer games, nothing more. But I indicated these. 'There's the answer to C.T.,' I said to her. And I watched her metamorphose, Magda, beautiful Christophine metamorphosing into what she really was. Then she took her pretty ivory delectro and fired into the flexium computer leads. There was a tolerably bloody bang. When I came to, the sprinklers were on. Christophine had taken the plastase reels and run. The lab was in quite a mess. And I—you saw what was left of me, in my capsule.

"Christ, it's getting hard to—talk, Magda. Better hurry it up. There was an emergency med-kit in the wall. The analgens numbed the burns sufficiently so that I could get out of the unit, get my car and drive to the jet-sheds. I realized that I couldn't move anywhere but off the island, if I wanted to go on living. And I did want to live, Magda. I did, very much. She must have waited for me in my apartment some hours. She'd reacted hastily. She couldn't be certain I was dead. She hadn't dared fire at me direct, it would have shown up as a murder—but an energy-surge in a malfunctioning lead—they occur. In the end, she came back to the unit, and I wasn't there, and then I suppose she tried out the plastase reels and learned about her big mistake. She'd made another mistake, too. She'd left the genetic blueprints, hers and mine, behind in the lab. And I'd taken them with me. The point is, I'd erased the answer to C.T. from the computer, but I'd still read it through beforehand. I carried it in my brain. And she knew that, Magda. And she knew what I'd do next. But not how, or where. Or when.

"Three years. She must have been on edge every day for this to happen, for you to walk in through her door. Poor Christa. Perhaps the irony appealed to her somewhat—that I'd tried to prevent C.T. from ever being used, that she'd forced me to—use it."

Claudio's voice had grown slurred. Sometimes his words were mispronounced; at first he would try to correct them, but gradually he stopped trying, since it wasted time.

"Being rich has so many advantages. False I.D. when things are hot. Nice friendly bribes to fan out the fires. Enough cash to hold up out of sight. To prepare the capsule, rig the Transfer. Difficult. It was—difficult. No help. Everything to be done first hand. And all the while the pain—or else so doped with analgens I could barely remember who I was. But I did it, Magda. And all I had to do after that was find—someone like you—who'd jump at the chance of a—of a new exquisite body. Christophine's exquisite body. I—wanted to *show* her, just how a simulate could be *misused*. Magda," he said. His voice was suddenly scored by terror. "Can't see you anymore. Are you still there, Magda?"

"Yes," she said.

"You'll have noticed she was more thorough with me. Every lead broken. The oxygen cut off. Able to repair, but not properly. Awash with the fucking slime-green toxic now. Suitable, applicable poison. She had it ready in her car when she went to Saint Azoro, hunting for me. Handy for her tonight. Magda, are you there?"

"Yes."

"I knew you'd meet her. Reckoned you'd attempt to kill her—no, maybe, I didn't. But on this occasion—kill her. She's got the panel. She can get the answer to C.T. from the panel. She may already have—no, she won't go to the unit now. She'll do it tomorrow, front of everyone. Kudos. Kill her, Magda, do you hear me?"

"Yes."

"Magda, I'm afraid to die. I wish I weren't. Kill her, Magda. Ditch her body. Become Christophine. Then leave. Who'll stop you? You're her. It's easy. Easy if macabre. She's rich. Your prints are hers. Do you hear me, Magda? Kill her for her money. Not for me. Astrads. Do you hear?'

"Claudio," she said.

"Oh, God, I'm scared," he said. "I'm scared, Magda."

"Claudio," she said. She put her arms about him though it hardly mattered, he could neither see her nor feel her grasp on him.

It was not even Claudio she held. Not truly Claudio.

And then the burned anaesthetized thing in the capsule must have died, for what she held slackened and collapsed inside her arms. There was, of course, no last breath.

Magdala climbed the metal road, between the vast stems of the trees, as the flaring jewel-colors of the storm bled out of them.

She climbed slowly, exhaustedly. It did not aid her to

recall that this body could not, in itself, experience fatigue. She experienced fatigue.

Rose and mauve and cerise and green, the jewels trickled down the stems of the trees. Daffodil, violet, and blue.

Presently, the forest became black. Sheer black.

The electric forest.

Nothing is to be relied on. The forest is not real. Its fires are not. Magdala is not. Nor Claudio.

Claudio.

Nothing is to be relied on.

Nothing is what it seems.

After two hours, she reached the columen bungalow, which, like the forest, had reverted to darkness.

Are you asleep, Christophine? Or awake? You can't keep me out. Your doors are open to me.

The garage accepted the print of her thumb, and let her in. She pressed for the elevator. The elevator came and bore her upward.

She moved into the bungalow, which had no lights, not even a solitary lamp.

Magdala went softly. To the glazium chimney whose flame had been switched off, to the swinging couch where Claudio had lain upon her, to the kitchen of knives—which she did not touch. The bathroom was vacant.

She expects me. She understands—somehow—that I may not have died and that I may seek her.

Or Claudio. She may expect Claudio. As before.

She is in the solarium.

Magdala reached the elevator. The elevator rose. Five seconds. The solarium.

Darkness. Dark Glass. Overhead, a mulberry star, a star like green mint-candy. Black paper rustling: plants.

Christophine.

Christophine burst from the dark. Green dazzle, mulberry dazzle on the blade of a knife. The delectro was in the sea. What else but a knife?

The knife slit the air. Magdala caught the wrist with the knife. With her free hand she raised her own weapon high, and plunged the syringe, one third full of poison, into the neck of Christophine, into the vein which led to the heart of Christophine.

Then stood there as Christophine, sprawled among black paper leaves, kicked, contorted, lay quivering, lay dead.

And now I am Christophine.

In the garage below was Christophine's car. Tomorrow, she would put the body of Christophine in the car. She would switch the car to robot-drive, and let it drive itself into the coruscating sea.

Tomorrow, and tomorrow, and tomorrow.

I am Christophine.

She went down in the elevator and stepped out into the bungalow. She walked across the large open-plan room to the northern window-wall, and raised the two lids of the contrachorda.

Seated in the dark, and weeping, she began to play Sadrès' "Variations on a Theme by Prokofiev."

Post-Screening Sonogram

THE CONSCIOUSNESS TRANSFERRAL Project was begun on Earth ten years ago, and as so often happens, the ethics of such a venture were not considered until the breakthrough had been achieved. By this time the Conclave was well aware that several other Federation governments had underway similar if not identical projects, and that what had begun as a race toward a medical miracle that would put an end to the savagery of particular types of replacement surgery, had now become an enterprise of paramount interest to the espionage networks of the Outer Worlds.

A program of study of the non-medical uses and effects of C.T. was therefore proposed, a project that was to be code-named Antipholus. As controller of this program, I quickly began to doubt the validity of any kind of study that was not based on actual living experiment. I was sufficiently convinced of this to suggest the gargantuan scheme that was, one year later, put into operation on the E.C. pre-colony planet Indigo Nine.

At first glance, to take an entire world off the map, put it out of bounds to legitimate traffic, and proceed to utilize it purely as a testing area seems riotously extravagant. And no doubt it is. However, Indigo Nine, though a lovely world in terms of its appearance, had not yet been opened up to popular colonization. Small, infertile save in nonedible flora, and lean in mineral deposits and uranium, without even a natural satellite to facilitate space-docking, Indigo had little to offer save room and privacy—which two properties were more necessary to Antipholus than any other thing. The erected city and surrounding plants and stations, part of a colony preparation plan but not yet occupied, proved invaluable. To build up the picture of a logically exploited world was an alarming task, in view of the fact that the total personnel of the Antipholus Program numbered only six hundred.

Having acquired the location, the subject—or protagonist—of the experiment was due to be selected. At this juncture, I caused a furor by proposing myself. There were the usual arguments—that my job was to sit at the helm of the ship, to monitor and to guide but not to become enmeshed. I in turn argued that nobody in the Antipholus Program could fail to become enmeshed. That with a mere six hundred men and women at our disposal, no one could very well avoid participation. And, in fact, to his eternal credit, Paul has proved my point, by combining the role of acting Program Controller in my stead, with that of a chief figure in the drama itself.

I also contend that I was the best bet as guinea pig, though we had no shortage of volunteers. Live experiment of such a nature, with a human subject, is a chancy thing. I kept my sanity and I got where I meant to go, but there were no guarantees at any time. Having invented the rules, I believe I was both entitled and obligated to abide by them myself. I wanted to place no other in a position of such danger. That I survived is largely due to the skill of others, and particularly to my husband, who had the unnerving work of systematically mentally torturing me while striving, of necessity unnoticed, to safeguard my wits. That Claudio, the gentlest and most stable of men, undertook this horrific labor is a miracle in itself. I cannot commend his efforts too highly. I know that he thought that I had already gone quite mad when I proposed myself as the experimental subject. He spent three months of Deks attempting to dissuade me. When that failed, he proposed himself as the co-subject, the essential Pygmalion figure of the drama. And, in one vital way, of course, Claudio was a godsend. Not a scientist but an accomplished professional actor, he could carry that taxing and terrifying persona with a genius that elicited the definitive responses. I doubt if anyone else could have supported me under the circumstances. I probably would have gone mad, and the Program failed. It was Claudio, incidentally, who christened the project "Antipholus"—from the sixteenth Earth-century Shakespearian play *The Comedy of Errors*. Indeed, a suitable title, for the play deals with two sets of doubles, of whom the twin brothers Antipholus "could not be distinguished but by name."

To describe then the background to the live experiment, its raison d'être and its modus operandi.

Our information leads us to suppose that the Outer Worlds will seek to remove—or simply upstage—certain important men and women in the Conclave, substituting their doubles—simulate bodies motivated by the transferred consciousness of Out-Conclave spies, saboteurs, and even assassins. In order to be prepared against this threat, we need to understand its scope, and its limitations, where the vulnerable spots are to be found, the give-aways, and the emotional levers. We also need, in honesty, to have our own version of the threat marshaled in readiness. And therefore we have to comprehend what pitfalls our own people may have to negotiate when transferred to an alien androidous body—to all intents and purposes their own. And—crowning perplexity—how they will cope with the possibility of coming face to face with their own replicates, those they are impersonating: the eternal question of alter-ego, mirror-image, and self-worshiping Narcissus beside the pool.

The only solution, given this batch of dismayingly complicated questions was, or so I assert, to invent a reasonably plausible set of events, all of which would, in various ways, illuminate those aspects we had to learn about. In fact, to invent a play, then assemble a troupe to act it out from inception to climax. With, in the lead, one person—the subject of C.T.—who must completely believe what was happening, and thus demonstrate, unvarnished, the answers to the questions.

The Outer-Worlds have displayed a primitive religious bias against the Conclave norm of pre-birth selection match. Coupled to unfavorable conditions in many decentralized settlements on these worlds, random conception has led to a high birth rate of deformed and crippled children. It now appears that it is these unfortunates, grown to adulthood, who will be, and are, approached by the spy networks, and offered the liberation of a physically sound body. Not many are likely to refuse. Furthermore, the minds are generally as crippled as the bodies by the mid-twenties, for they are gracelessly treated by their peers, often actually attacked, or at best, pilloried in more subtle fashion. Having developed in frustration, jealousy, bitterness, and hatred, and given sudden physical liberty, followed by network training and an outlet, these impulses to destruction could become extraordinary and potentially ab-human.

Again, our sources of information lead us to the conclusion that in each case, a "mentor" will be used, a single man or woman of powerful personality and sexual attraction, who will contact the subjects in the initial stage, and remain with them thereafter in the capacity, literally, of a sort of evil genius, urging them toward whatever goal the network has allocated them. We do not know positively what shape the training will take, but we suspect the mentor will pass on to the subject a loathing of whomever he or she is to supplant. There is also the chance that the mentor will be a specially handpicked traitor from the Conclave, someone who, for personal reasons, wishes to harm the simulate's victim. The traitor, suffering himself from a love-hate compulsion toward his victim, will work out his distractions upon the transfer subject who has come to resemble the victim.

As you see, I describe the basic substance of the Magdala-Claudio-Christophine relationship. Indeed, it was as close an imitation as one could foster. Claudio's mentoral sadism, vacillation, and neurasthenic insecurity were all extensions of his position as the hate-love ridden traitor figure. The effect of his moods upon the subject was startling—masochistic obedience offset by flashes of sinister rebellion. Insanity rubs off, it seems, in such a dualogue.

Seduction will also be an accepted ingredient in the relationship. The mentor will seduce the transfer subject in order to bind the emotional cords more tightly. For obvious reasons, the subject's experience of sex will be, as a crippled Out-Worlder, impoverished. Other parallels—the element of intrigue (Paul's deal with Christophine, the recorder in the bracelet, etc.), the penetration of an alien zone (Two Unit and Marine Bleu), were introduced as specifically as possible. By use of the disastrous Two Unit C. T. Project, we were also able to determine the subject's reaction, objectively, to her own condition. Whereas, in the final sequence (the revelation of Claudio's capsule), we postulate that we have unearthed the greatest emotive lever that can be used against a subject. However, these points must so far remain moot.

To turn to the hypnotic technique of the experiment.

The format employed was that of mind-erase, coupled to the restorative of mnemonic recall. This is a precarious gambit, additionally so because it had perforce to be interrupted, in my case, by a memory implant—the grisly childhood and adult memories of Magdala Cled. (Again, I owe a whole mind to others, from whom one slip could have meant appalling loss to my mental process.) I was also endowed with Magdala's hate-potential, her high and constant fear level, her inverted personality, and sexually deprived and wasted spirit. Last, but hardly least, knowledge of Indigo as a colony-development planet, Class Three, the same as twenty or so Conclave planets on the same rung of the ladder. Doramel and Irlin are responsible for the background details of Indigo. Again, praise seems inadequate. Uncountable touches show their creative flair—the seven-hundred vehicle car-park space at Sugar Beach, for example, and the dance floor sea-funnel in the restaurant. Or the dreadful cottene overalls of the City Processory. Everything designed as meticulously as the stage set which it had to serve for; actual settings, and mentally "recollected" ones, like the M.C. church of Magdala's orphanage. Crowd management, too, has called forth astonishing deeds. Recorded sound and holostetic effects have helped. About six hundred persons, to be deployed as a cast of thousands, is a stupendous barrier to scale. Paul has handled our "extras" with the finesse of the Tri-V director.

The last step over into the dark was my own brief experience of C.T.—three days in all. For, obviously, in this instance, the deformed body of Magdala was the constructed doll into which I was C.T. oriented at the start of the drama, and out of which I escaped—not to a construct, but back into my own genuine skin. To convince me thereafter that the human live body I existed in was an *androidous simulate* was no mean feat on the part of the Antipholus team. Injections of eliminex, which temporarily takes over from the bodily functions, were given to me during sleep, along with food concentrates, stimulants, and other drugs necessary to the deception. My drunk at Sugar Beach was induced by a high-alcohol preparation in my drinks, while other apparently alcoholic beverages were non-intoxicant synthetics. My periodic drugged sleeps were brought about by narrow-radius odorless gas. This was managed with exceptional finesse on my return to the vacant bungalow after my sojourn in Two Unit. On this occasion, the gas capsule was in the floor underlay and cracked when I trod on it. Such gas has no "hangover."

The requirement that I think Claudio had me robot-wired as a relay device was Paul's notion. He theorizes that such mechanics will be used in the subject transfer bodies. What will occur should the subject learn of it?

Everything, naturally, in this experiment was used to test a reaction, from my "mentor's" seduction of me to the sight of Emilion in Two Unit. The ultimate test, demonstrably, was my confrontation with Christophine.

Christophine deserves her own explanatory paragraphs. To begin with, the team's joint decision that I become a simulate of my actual true life self. Under mind-erase, theoretically this had no relevance, since all recollection of my original self was wiped away. (In fact, no names were altered, nor were any unfitting bells rung.) However, just as the mentor's sadistic tendencies were emphasized deliberately to overbalance the mentor-subject relationship, so a deeply subconscious link to Christophine—my own self—was used to overbalance my reply to her. We calculate that, should there be a meeting between absolute doubles (different from twins of any known variety, where minor differences are always present), a psycho-physical link will evolve.

Self-love is neither fantasy nor vulgar joke. The totality of the "I," the inbuilt survival and self-protective trait, is one of the most unshakable syndromes known to psycho-science. We are, if you like, pre-programmed to put ourselves first in eight out of ten psycho-analytic situations. Exact doubles, until now, have never been envisaged. To kill that way is a suicide committed while staring in a mirror. That Christophine is truly myself, was a bonus turn of the screw on the enigma, which yielded unnerving data. Even Christophine's betrayal of her did not sufficiently influence Magdala. It took the discovery that Claudio was one of her own kind (the disclosure of the capsule) to overcome her prejudice. Claudio's death was used to cement Magdala's emotional reversal, while the revelation of Christophine's villainy was a coda to the elements of intrigue introduced before.

"Christophine" was, of course, an androidous-robot, controlled and directed from an area half a kilometer west of the bungalow. Again, an extravagance, but we did not intend to risk a second C.T. subject in a simulate of *my* body. My false confrontation was sufficient to cope with.

There remains a résumé of props. To begin, the abundant use of holostets in the drama. There was a reason for this, the spurious veracity of events to be propped up further by a medley of external, frankly unreal, symbols. Maybe you know the Cassandran story of the gloie and the dog. The dog determined to catch the gloie, who regularly stole poultry from the yard. But the gloie always saw the dog coming and ran. So one night, the dog stuck up three bundles of feathers in the yard, and dressed himself in a fourth. Along came the gloie and bit the first bunch of feathers—no good. Then the gloie bit the second; same thing. By now the gloie was wise. The feathers didn't move. Just then up strolled the dog, covered in feathers. "It moves," said the gloie, "ergo, it's a bird." The gloie accordingly ran at the dog and that was the end of the gloie. The holostetic trees were sprinkled around the mise en scène with a similar subcutaneous intention. Even so, the analogy of the electric forest has not passed us by.

Additional props and fakes worth mentioning include the energy charge in Christophine's delectro, which was obviously rigged, and the "genetic reprint" body of Christophine in the pillar at Claudio's house, which was the androidous-robot subsequently used as the "real" Christophine in Marine Bleu. Claudio's non-scientific lecture on C.T. was based on accurate data referring to a simulate construct. The maintenance capsules and their contents were dummies (Claudio is decidedly no simulate). Emilion at Two Unit, both static and active, was a dummy, in the latter case on a Tri-V film. The fish caught at Sugar Beach was a psycho-symbol of entrapment for Magdala, and was made of Plastase. The spin game in the Casino was rigged to gauge her feelings on winning—and also at losing.

Marine Bleu itself is a pre-built station, due to house oceanic biological study-groups. Sugar Beach is a pre-built hotel owned by the Danzig Corporation. All other goods, from paper books to autobuses, were the loan of various E.C. government departments.

That hypnotic black-outs and wake-ups, complete with bridge "memories," were used on Magdala to save time, is clear from a close reading of the text. And such a blackout was used during C.T. of myself as Magdala from the crippled simulate back to my own body. The eliminex lozenge which Claudio gave me in my "ugly" phase, was a placebo, designed merely to conceal from me that my current crippled body was the simulate and without bodily functions.

And one intriguing psychological detail. Magdala, as

a simulate Christophine, exhibits an exotic variety and self-aggrandizement amounting to distortion. Not only does she shut out all personalities, other than her own and Claudio's, Paul when he becomes a menace, and Christophine as an extension of self, she reduces the striking good looks of others to "flavorless" (the actual word "flavorless" registers on the tel-tapes). As for the eyes of Val Valary, I would stress that they are of normal size and luster. It appears even our optical process is colored by mental attitude.

The whole Antipholus Program was prepared, carried through, recorded, and assessed by an ingenious and honorable team. Without this team, the experiment would never have supplied the material which it has. Blow by blow analysis of the content is available via audio, optocon, and tel-tape cipher. But for the purposes of this sonogram, little more has to be said.

Since the completion of the experiment, we are able to counter the menace from the Outer Worlds with some confidence. We have now as much "live" experience of the simulate phenomena as they. And maybe more.

For example, we know, without a doubt, the answer to that apocalyptic question—that the subject can, given certain circumstances, be primed to kill its own image.

And that is the question upon which all further questions hang.

As subject and protagonist, I can claim small credit, since my burden was unconscious and rested upon the shoulders of others.

For the roll-call of honor, I cite Irlin Vander Lis and Doramel Schur, Nada Millas and Val Valary, Paul Hovak, who had one of the toughest assignments, to play a major figure and at the same moment to coordinate the team from the wings. Finally, my husband, Claudio

Loro, without whom I believe both this project, and I myself, would have foundered utterly.

To these, and to all the others who ran this demanding and merciless course, my gratitude and my thanks.

Lastly. Claudio's "dying" tirade against the misuse of C.T. was by way of a cadenza on his part. Though in reference it hits hardest—in the actual world beyond the experiment—at the Outer Planetary networks, none of us on Antipholus are likely to forget it.

Perhaps, as a basis for a Charter of Ethics, it is not foolish to remember the make-believe death of a make-believe character in an illusory landscape—the inventor who destroyed his invention after foreseeing its own ability to destroy. In our place, we can hardly go backward, but neither should we ignore the nakedness of humanity before the huge-wheeled vehicle of progress. We have too much to give, and far too much to learn, to throw ourselves away.

                                        Christophine del Jan Loro.

For their work on the Indigo Live Experiment, the entire team of the Antipholus Program were awarded the E.C. Commendation De Luxe. Claudio Loro and Christophine del Jan Loro were each awarded the Stella D'Or.

Indigo has since been popularly colonized, and is now a Class Four planet of the Earth Conclave Federation.

Regarding the Outer Worlds, vigilance is strictly maintained.

CJ Cherryh
The Foreigner Novels

"Serious space opera at its very best by one of the leading
SF writers in the field today." —*Publishers Weekly*

"Her world building, aliens, and suspense rank among
the strongest in the whole SF field." —*Booklist*

To Order Call: 1-800-788-6262
www.dawbooks.com